'Have you ever experienced that before, Alice?'

'Experienced what?' she asked in a hoarse whisper.

Gabriel laughed under his breath. 'The grip of passion that makes you behave irrationally…'

'I prefer to trust reasoning and logic,' she managed to say.

'So that's a no…'

'If you recall…' She was close to snapping, because not only was he making her feel uncomfortable but he was enjoying himself. 'I did say to you when I took this job that I didn't want to talk about my private life!'

'Was that what we were doing? Talking about your private life?'

He stood up, flexed his muscles, debated whether to let this conversation go and just as quickly decided not to.

Why deny it? She roused his curiosity. She was so contained, so secretive whilst giving the impression of being straightforward, so unwilling to share even the smallest of confidences… W‌‍   g you wanted—in‌   s thoughts and emo‌   y to have a person

SEVEN SEXY SINS

The *true* taste of temptation!

From greed to gluttony, lust to envy,
these fabulous stories explore what seven sexy sins
mean in the twenty-first century!

Whether pride goes before a fall, or wrath leads to
a passion that consumes entirely, one thing is certain:
the road to true love has never been more enticing!

So you decide:

How can it be a sin when it feels so good?

Sloth—Cathy Williams

Lust—Dani Collins

Pride—Kim Lawrence

Gluttony—Maggie Cox

Greed—Sara Craven

Wrath—Maya Blake

Envy—Annie West

Seven titles by some of
Mills & Boon® Modern™ Romance's
most treasured and exciting authors!

TO SIN
WITH THE TYCOON

BY
CATHY WILLIAMS

Published in Great Britain 2015
by Mills & Boon, an imprint of Harlequin (UK) Limited,
Eton House, 18-24 Paradise Road, Richmond, Surrey, TW9 1SR

© 2015 Cathy Williams

ISBN: 978-0-263-24829-6

Harlequin (UK) Limited's policy is to use papers that are natural,
renewable and recyclable products and made from wood grown in
sustainable forests. The logging and manufacturing processes conform
to the legal environmental regulations of the country of origin.

Printed and bound in Spain
by Blackprint CPI, Barcelona

Cathy Williams is originally from Trinidad, but has lived in England for a number of years. She currently has a house in Warwickshire, which she shares with her three daughters, Charlotte, Olivia and Emma, and their pet cat, Salem. She adores writing romantic fiction, and would love one of her girls to become a writer— although at the moment she is happy enough if they do their homework and agree not to bicker with one another!

Recent titles by the same author:

THE ARGENTINIAN'S DEMAND
SECRETS OF A RUTHLESS TYCOON
ENTHRALLED BY MORETTI
HIS TEMPORARY MISTRESS

Did you know these are also available as eBooks?
Visit www.millsandboon.co.uk

To my beautiful daughters for all their support

CHAPTER ONE

ALICE MORGAN WAS growing more annoyed by the second. It was ten-thirty. She had now been sitting in this office for an hour and a half and no one could tell her whether she would be sitting there, tapping her foot and looking at her watch, for another hour and a half, two hours, three hours or for the rest of the day.

In fact, she seemed to have been forgotten. Mr Big played by his own rules, she had been told. He came and went as he pleased. He did as he wanted. He was unpredictable, a law unto himself. All this had been relayed to her by a simpering, pocket-sized blonde Barbie doll as she had been ushered into her office to find that her new boss was nowhere to be found.

'Perhaps he has a diary?' Alice had suggested. 'Maybe he had a breakfast meeting and forgot that I would be coming at nine. If you could check, then at least I would know how long I can expect to be kept waiting.'

But, no. Mr Big didn't run his life according to diaries. Apparently he didn't need to because he was so clever that he could remember everything without the benefit of reminders. Besides, no one was allowed into his office when he was absent—although the Barbie doll had worked for him for four days a few months ago and knew for a fact that he didn't use any diaries. Because he was brilliant and didn't need them.

The Barbie doll had since peered into the office twice, smiled apologetically and repeated what she had previously said—as though lateness and discourtesy were winning selling points that the entire staff happily accepted and so, therefore, should she.

Mouth tight, Alice looked around her, from her smaller office through the dividing glass partition into Gabriel Cabrera's much bigger, much more impressive one.

When she had been told where she would be temping, Alice had been thrilled. The offices were situated in the most stunning building in the city. The Shard was a testimony to architectural brilliance with magnificent views over London. People paid to go up it. The bars and restaurants there were booked up weeks in advance.

And now she would be working there. True, her contract was only for six weeks, but she had been told that there was a chance of being made permanent if she did well. He had a reputation for hiring and firing, the woman at the agency had added, but Alice was good at what she did. Better than good. By the time she'd arrived at the building at precisely eight-forty-five that morning, she had made up her mind that she would do her damnedest to secure a permanent position there.

Her last job had been pleasant and reasonably well paid, but the surroundings had been mediocre and the chances of advancement non-existent. This job, should she manage to get it, promised a career that might actually move in an upward direction.

Right now, she thought that she wouldn't be going anywhere if her new boss didn't show up, except back to her little shared house in Shepherd's Bush with one wasted day behind her. She probably wouldn't even be paid for her time because no one would sign off her work sheet if she didn't actually do any work. She wondered whether his reputation as a hirer and firer wasn't actually a case of him being left in the lurch every three weeks because his secretaries got fed up dealing with his so-called brilliance. Not so much a case of him firing his secretaries as his secretaries firing him.

She caught a glimpse of herself in the mirrored wall that occupied one section of her office and frowned at the image reflected back: her neat outfit and unremarkable looks did not seem to gel with the glossy, snappy image of the other employees she had seen as she had been channelled onto the directors' floor. She could have landed on a film set. The guys all wore snappy, expensive suits and the women were largely blonde and achingly good-looking in a polished, well-groomed way. Young, thrusting, career graduates who all had the full package of looks, ambition and brains. Even the secretaries and clerks who kept the wheels of the machinery oiled and running were just as glamorous. These were people who dressed for their surroundings.

She, on the other hand...

Brown eyes, brown hair falling straight to her shoulders, and she was far too tall, even in her flat, black pumps. Something about her grey suit and white blouse screamed lack of flair, although when she had stuck it on that morning she had been quietly pleased at the professional image she projected. It had certainly made a change from the more casual gear she had become accustomed to wearing at her last job. Now, here, she just looked vaguely...*drab*.

For the first time she wondered whether the gleaming CV in her handbag and her confidence in her abilities were going to be enough. An eccentric and insane employer who surrounded himself with glamour models might just find her a little on the boring side.

She swept aside the nudge of insecurity trying to push itself to the forefront. This wasn't a fashion parade and she wasn't competing with anyone in the looks stakes. This was a job, and she was good at what she did. She picked things up easily; she had an agile brain. When it came to work, those were the things that mattered.

She hunkered down for the long haul.

It was nearly midday, and she was bracing herself for an awkward conversation with one of his employees about his whereabouts, when the door to her office was pushed open.

And in he came. Her new boss, Gabriel Cabrera. And nothing had prepared her for him. Tall, well over six foot, he was the most sinfully good-looking man she had ever set eyes on. His hair was slightly too long, which lent him a rakish air, and the perfection of his dark, chiselled features was indecent. He emanated power and a sort of restless energy that left her temporarily lost for words. Then she gathered herself and held out her hand in greeting.

'Who are you?' Gabriel stopped abruptly and frowned at her. 'And why are you here?'

Alice dropped her hand and bared her teeth in a polite smile. This was the man she would be working for and she didn't want to kick things off on the wrong foot—but, in her head, she added to the list of pejorative descriptions which had been growing steadily 'rude and fancies himself'.

'I'm Alice Morgan…your new secretary? The agency your company uses got in touch with me. I have my CV…'

'No need.' He stood back and looked at her intently, head tilted to one side. Arms folded, he circled her, and she gritted her teeth in receipt of this insolent, arrogant appraisal.

Was this how he treated his female staff? She had got the message loud and clear that he did what he wanted, irrespective of what anyone had to say on the matter, but this was too much.

She could leave. Walk out. She had already been kept waiting for over two hours. The agency would understand. But she was being paid over the odds for this job, way over the odds, and it had been hinted that the package, should she be made permanent, would be breath-taking. The man paid well, whatever his undesirable traits, and she could do with the money. She had been renting for the past three years, ever since she had moved to London from Devon, where her mother lived. There was no way she could afford to leave rented accommodation but she would love to have the option of not sharing a house. And then there were all those other expenses that ate into her monthly income, leaving her with barely enough to survive comfortably.

Practicality won over impulse and she stayed put.

'So...' Gabriel drawled, eyebrows raised. 'My new secretary. Now that you mention it, I *was* expecting you.'

'I've been here since eight-forty-five.'

'Then you should have had ample opportunity to read and digest all the information on my various companies.' He nodded to the low ash sideboard which was home to various legal books and, yes, an abundance of financial reports on his companies. She had read them all cover to cover.

Alice felt her hackles rise. 'Perhaps,' she said, keeping her voice level, 'you could give me a run-down of my duties? Normally there's a handover from the old secretary to the new one but...' *But the last one obviously ran for cover without looking back...*

'I don't actually have time to run through every detail of what you're expected to do. You'll just have to pick it up as you go along. I'm assuming the agency will have sent me someone competent who doesn't need too much hand-holding.' He watched as delicate colour invaded her cheeks. Her eyes were very firmly averted from him and she was as stiff as a piece of board.

All told, it was not the reaction Gabriel usually expected or received from the opposite sex, but perhaps the agency had been right to send him someone who wouldn't end up with an inappropriate crush on him. Miss Alice Morgan— and she looked every bit a 'Miss' even if he hadn't known she was—clearly had her head very firmly screwed on.

'Item number one on the agenda is…a cup of coffee. You'll find that that's an essential duty. I like mine strong and black with two sugars. If you unbend slightly and turn to the left, you'll notice a sliding door. All coffee making facilities are there.'

So far, everything the man was saying was getting on her nerves, and she hadn't missed the amusement in his voice when he had told her that she could 'unbend'.

'Of course.'

'Then you can grab your computer and come into my office. Fire it up and we can get going. I have some big deals on the go. You might find that you're being thrown in at the deep end. And you can relax, Miss Morgan. I don't eat secretaries for breakfast.'

Her legs finally started moving as he disappeared into his office. Duty number one : coffee making. She had not made coffee for her boss in her last job. There, everyone had chipped in. Quite frequently, Tom Davis had been the one bringing *her* a cup of coffee. It was clear that Gabriel Cabrera did not operate on such civilised lines.

By nature, Alice was not confrontational. There was, however, a streak of fierce independence in her that railed against his dictatorial attitude. She simmered and seethed as she made the coffee for him.

His image still swam in her head with pressing insistence: that ridiculously sexy face; the casual assumption that he was the big boss and so could do precisely as he pleased, even if his behaviour bordered on rude. He was rich, he was drop-dead good-looking and he knew the full extent of the power he wielded. When he had stood in front of her, she had felt as vulnerable as a minnow in the presence of a shark. Something about him was suffocating, larger than life. He was dressed in a suit, charcoal-grey, but even that had not been able to conceal the breadth of his shoulders or the lean muscularity of his physique.

He was a man who was far, far too good-looking, far too overpowering.

'Sit,' was his first word as she entered the hallowed walls of his office.

It was a vast space. Floor-to-ceiling panes of glass flooded the room with natural light which was kept at bay by pale-grey shutters. Beyond the immediate vicinity of his working area was a sectioned-off space in which low chairs circled a table and tall plants created a semi-private meeting space.

'You'd better brief me very quickly on what computer systems you're familiar with.' He drummed a fountain pen on his desk, which was chrome and glass, and gave her his undivided attention.

A sparrow. Neat as a pin, legs primly pressed together, eyes tactfully managing to avoid eye contact. Gabriel wondered whether he should send her back in exchange for something a little more decorative. He liked decorative, even though he knew the drawbacks always outweighed the advantages. But, hell, he was a man who could have anything he wanted at the click of a finger and that included interchangeable secretaries. Ever since Gladys—his sixty-year-old assistant of seven years—had inconsiderately emigrated to Australia to be with her daughter, he had run through temps like water. He knew that any agency worth its salt would have scratched him from their books if he'd been anyone else, just as he knew that they never would with him. He paid so well that they would be saying farewell to far too much commission and, in the end, wasn't greed at the bottom of everything?

His lips curled in derision. Was there nothing he couldn't have? There were definite upsides to being able to get whatever he wanted... Women flocked to him; heads of business fell silent when he spoke; the press followed him with bated breath, waiting for a hint of the next financial scoop or for a glimpse of his very active private life. He was at the very peak of his game, the undisputed leader of the pack, and there were no signs that he would be relinquishing the position any time soon. So why did life sometimes feel so damned *unsatisfying*?

He sometimes wondered whether he had used up his capacity for any genuine emotion in his tenacious climb to the top. Perhaps battling against the odds had actually been the great adventure. Now that the game had been played and he had emerged the winner, was the adventure over? Not even the brutal, frenetic push and shove of work could provide him with the adrenaline it once did. What was the point of trying when you could have it all without effort? Was *trying* just something else that had once mattered but now no longer did in the same way?

The sparrow was in full flow, telling him about her last job and giving him a long list of her responsibilities there. He held up one imperious hand, stopping her mid-sentence.

'You can only be an improvement on the last girl,' he drawled. 'I think somewhere along the line the agency lost track of the fact that I actually wanted someone who knew how to type using more than one finger.'

Alice smiled politely and thought that maybe the agency was in the dark as to whether he cared one way or another, given that his priorities seemed to lie with how good-looking the candidates were.

Gabriel frowned at that smile; it seemed at odds with the meek and mild exterior projected. 'You'll find the file on the Hammonds deal on your computer,' he said, focusing now. 'Call it up and I'll tell you what you need to do.'

Alice didn't surface for the next four hours. Gabriel kept her pinned to her computer. There was no lunch break, because it had been practically lunchtime when he had eventually strolled into the office, and he clearly assumed that she would not be hungry. He wasn't, after all, so why should she be?

At four-thirty, she looked up to find him standing in front of her.

'You seem to be keeping up. New broom sweeping clean, or can I expect this show of efficiency to be on-going?'

Under the full impact of his rapid-fire instructions, Alice had forgotten how objectionable she found him. If that was his way of telling her that she had done a good job on day one, then surely there had to be more polite ways of delivering the message?

'I'm a hard worker, Mr Cabrera,' she told him evenly. 'I can usually handle what's thrown at me.'

Gabriel sat down in the chair facing her desk and extended his long legs to one side.

Every inch of him breathed self-assurance and command. Okay, so she had to admit that the man was clever. He had the astute brain of a lawyer and an ability to pick through the finer details until he found the essential make or break one that was the difference between success and failure. On the telephone, he was confident and authoritative. From every pore of his body, he radiated the self-assurance that what he wanted, he would get.

'Highly commendable,' he said drily.

'Thank you. Perhaps you could tell me what time I shall be expected to work until today?' *Considering he had kept her waiting for hours for reasons he had not bothered to share.*

'Until I'm satisfied that your job for the day is done,' Gabriel said coolly. 'I don't believe in clock watching, Miss Morgan. Unless, of course, you have some pressing need to go by five? Have you?'

Alice smoothed her skirt with nervous hands. She had read all the promotional literature on offer during the three-hour wait in her office, and within a few seconds had known that the man was beyond influential. He was a billionaire with killer looks and she had seen from the way he had dealt with various interruptions by staff members during the day that, as the little Barbie had informed her, he did exactly as he pleased. One poor woman, the head of his legal department, had been told very firmly that she would be required to work the following weekend without a break because they were closing an important deal and would therefore be required to miss her best friend's wedding. He hadn't even bothered to pay lip service to an apology.

Gabriel Cabrera paid his employees the earth and in return they handed over their freedom.

That was a bandwagon Alice had no intention of jumping on. Right now, she was nothing more than a lowly temp, so could speak her mind and lay down some boundaries. Because should—and it was a big should—the job be offered to her on a permanent basis, then she would no longer have the freedom to tell him what she was willing to do and what she wasn't. And working weekends was definitely not on the agenda. Not given her mother's current situation.

'I'm not a clock watcher, Mr Cabrera, and I'm more than happy to work overtime if necessary. But, yes, I do value my private life and I would have to know in advance if I'm expected to sacrifice my leisure time.'

Gabriel looked at her narrowly. 'That's not how my company operates.' Indeed, that was not how *he* operated. Doling out long explanations for what he did was not part of the package. He did as he pleased and the world accepted it. He felt another tug of weary cynicism which he swatted aside. He had earned his place at the head of the table by fighting off the competition. He had started from nothing and now had everything...and that had been the object of the game: to have it all. He was accountable to no one, least of all a secretary who had been with him for two minutes!

'If I understand correctly, you're being paid double what you would normally get doing the same job in another company.'

But with a different boss, Alice was tempted to insert. *A* normal *boss.*

'That's true,' she admitted.

'Are you going to tell me that you don't like the nice, juicy pay packet? Because I can, of course, slash it if you want to start imposing conditions for your working hours. You've been here for five minutes and you think that you can start dictating terms?' He gave a short, incredulous laugh and shook his head. 'Unbelievable.'

'The agency implied that there might be a permanent job on offer if I made it through the probation period. I understand you haven't had a great deal of success with the previous secretaries who were sent to you.'

'And, because you've had a good first day, you somehow think that you have leverage?' But he had had a bad time of it when it came to his secretaries. Perhaps he should have been hunting down a Plain Jane like the one sitting in front of him, but you should be able to get along with the person in whose company you usually ended up spending most of your day. That seemed a sensible conclusion. He was forced to concede that his theory fell down slightly given the fact that some of the girls he had employed had wanted to get along a little too well with him for his liking.

'You seem to be getting a little ahead of yourself here,' he remarked, watching her closely. 'Wouldn't you agree?'

'No.' Alice took a deep breath, prepared to stand her ground, because she could see very clearly how the land lay with this guy.

Dark eyes clashed with hazel and she felt a tremendous whoosh go through her, as though the air had been sucked out of her body. She found him unnerving, yet today had been the most invigorating she had spent in a long time. She had blossomed under the pressure of her workload, had even seen areas where she might be able to branch out and assume more responsibility.

Was she willing to jeopardise six weeks of a sure thing in favour of laying down ground rules for a permanent job that might not even be hers?

Even as she asked herself that question, she knew the answer. She wasn't going to let anyone, however much they were paying her, dictate the parameters of her life, and not just her working life. No one in his company seemed to mind. Half the women were probably besotted with him, but not her, and she needed her time out. Life was difficult enough as it was, with her weekends taken up going to Devon to visit her mother. The last thing she needed was to have her precious week-day evenings sucked away, even if it meant forfeiting paid overtime.

'I beg your pardon?' Gabriel couldn't actually recall the last time anyone had ventured an opinion that was obviously unwelcome. Great wealth gave great freedom, and commanded even greater respect, and hadn't that always been his driving goal in life—to jettison the dark days of growing up in foster homes, where his opinion had counted for nothing and his life had been in the control of other people?

'I've only been here for one day, Mr Cabrera, and on my first day I waited for nearly three hours until you arrived. Yes, that *did* give me ample time to read your company literature, but I wasn't aware that that would be how I would spend my morning.'

'Are you asking me to account for my whereabouts this morning?' He looked at her with blatant incredulity.

At this juncture ordinarily, she would have ambushed all her chances of having another day in his company, much less the permanent position she seemed to think might be hers. But he was galled to discover that the thought of another line of inept secretaries inconveniently fancying him was not appealing, even if he *did* enjoy the pleasant view from his office they provided.

He was also weirdly fascinated by her nerve.

'Of course I'm not! And I do realise that it's not my place to start laying down any terms and conditions...'

'But you're going to anyway?' Blazing anger was only just kept in check by the fact that she had done damn well on the work front, too well to dismiss without a back-up waiting in the wings.

'I'm afraid I can't sacrifice my weekends working for you, Mr Cabrera.'

'I don't believe I asked you to.'

'No, but I saw you cancel that poor girl's weekend. Her best friend's wedding, and you told her that she had no choice but to work solidly here on both days.'

'Claire Kirk makes a very big deal about being one of the youngest in the company to head a department. She's good at what she does, and it would be a mistake to encourage her into thinking that she'll go places in this company if she isn't prepared to go the extra mile.'

Alice didn't say anything but she wondered whether he knew that there was 'going the extra mile' and then there was sacrificing your life for the sake of a *job*.

'I wouldn't have made a big deal about any of this,' she said quietly, 'But I thought you ought to know how I feel about my working conditions from day one rather than not say anything and then find myself expected to work hours I'm not willing to work. I'm not saying that I won't do overtime now and again, but I'm a firm believer in separating my personal life from my working life.'

'Tell me something, did you lay down similar boundary lines for your last boss?'

'I didn't have to,' she replied.

'Because he was a nine-to-five-thirty kind of guy? Thought so. Well, I'm not a nine-to-five-thirty kind of guy and I don't expect my employees to be nine-to-five-thirty kind of people.' It would be a shame to lose someone who showed potential but he had humoured her for long enough. 'Employees like Claire, who want to aggressively climb career ladders, work weekends when they don't want to because they understand the rules of the game. The prize never goes to the person who doesn't realise that a little sacrifice is necessary now and again if something important arises. Granted, you're not the head of a department, and you may not want any kind of career to speak of—'

'I *do* want to have a career!' Bright patches of colour appeared on her cheeks.

'Really? I'm all ears, because you're not selling it…'

Alice licked her lips nervously and stared at him. There was a brooding stillness to him that was unsettling. Nerves did their best to launch her into mindless chatter but a deeply ingrained habit of keeping her private life to herself held her back and she composed herself sufficiently to flash him another of her polite smiles.

'That was why I left my last job. I liked it there but Tom, the director of the company, was going to hand the reins over to his son, and Tom Junior wasn't a strong believer in women in the workplace, especially not in the haulage business.'

Gabriel cocked his head to one side, listening to what she was saying and what she wasn't. She talked like a prissy school-marm but there was nothing prissy or school-marmish about the way she had stood up for herself. She claimed to want a career but, when pressed, could only tell him something vague about why she had left her last company. Given half a chance, most women couldn't wait to involve him in long stories about themselves, especially long stories that were slanted in their favour, but this one… He got the feeling that she only said what she wanted someone to hear and that included him.

He glanced over her, his eyes taking in the unimaginative get-up, the long, slim frame, the uninspiring haircut.

His employees were all given a generous clothes allowance. They could afford designer gear, and this worked in particular favour of his staff lower down the pecking order, whose salaries were less enviable. Everyone, whatever their ranking, projected a certain image and he liked that. Compared to them, the little sparrow in front of him lacked polish, but there was something about her…

'So what were you planning your career to be there, had little Tommy Junior not come along to fill Daddy's shoes…?' Gabriel had virtually no respect for anyone gifted a business. He had had to find his way by walking on broken glass and he was fundamentally contemptuous of all those well- groomed, pampered boys and girls born with silver spoons in their mouths. He was a hard man who had travelled a hard road. It had worked well for him, had put him where he was today, able to do precisely as he pleased.

'I thought I might be able to get funding for an accountancy course…' She thought wistfully of the dreams she had once had to get involved in finance. She had always had a thing for numbers and it had seemed a lucrative and satisfying road to go down. Dreams, she had discovered, had a tendency to remain unfulfilled. Or at least, hers had.

'It wasn't to be,' she said briskly. 'So I thought that perhaps joining a bigger, more ambitious company might be a good idea.'

'But, before you got too accustomed to the job, you felt it necessary to tell me that your working schedule is limited.'

'My weekends are accounted for.' Alice was beginning to wish that she had decided never to say anything. She should have just kept her head down and then crossed whatever bridge she had to cross when she came to it. Instead, she had made assumptions about the way he ran his company and had decided to act accordingly.

'Boyfriend?'

'I beg your pardon?'

'Or maybe husband, although I don't see any wedding ring on the finger.'

'Sorry, but what are you talking about?'

'Isn't it usually the boyfriend in the background who

ends up dictating the working hours?' Gabriel asked, intrigued by her outspokenness, her sheer gall in laying down ground rules on day one—as though she had any right—with *him*. Intrigued, too, by that air of concealment that was so unusual in a woman. At least, in the women he knew.

'Not in this case, Mr Cabrera,' Alice told him stiffly.

'No boyfriend?'

Alice hesitated but, perhaps having misjudged her timing to start with, why not go the whole hog and expand on her conditions? He would probably chuck her out on the spot. She would return to the agency, who wouldn't be surprised to see her, and they would find her another job—something with a normal boss, working normal hours in a normal environment. It sounded unappetising.

'I should mention…' She heard the wooden formality in her voice and cringed because she was twenty-five years old, yet she sounded like someone twice her age. 'I also do not appreciate talking about my personal life.'

'Why not? Have you got something to hide?'

Alice's mouth fell open and, in return, Gabriel raised his eyebrows without bothering to help her out of her awkward silence.

'I…I do a very good job. I take my work very seriously. If you decide to keep me on, you won't regret it, Mr Cabrera. I bring one hundred and ten percent to everything I do in the working environment…'

Gabriel didn't say anything. He watched her flounder and wondered whether she brought one hundred and ten percent to whatever it was she did in the leisure time that she was so stridently protecting.

'Accountancy courses require weekend time… What would you do about those precious weekends of yours that you can't possibly sacrifice?'

'I can do the work in my own time,' Alice said promptly. 'I've checked it out. And I would pass the exams. I have a good head for figures.'

'In which case, remind me why you didn't go into that field of work when you left school…college…university? In fact, now that you seem to be campaigning for a permanent job with me, why don't you hand over the CV which I am sure is burning a hole in your bag…?'

Alice hesitated fractionally and Gabriel looked at her, his dark eyes cool and assessing.

His mobile phone rang; he glanced down at the caller ID and then he, too, hesitated, fractionally, but this time there was a smile hovering on his lips as he disconnected the call.

'Here's the deal, Miss Morgan.' He sat forward, invading her space, and rested his elbows on her desk.

Alice automatically inched back and her breathing quickened as their eyes clashed. Suddenly, she was aware of every inch of her body in ways she had never been before. She felt hot all over; her breasts felt prickly and sensitive, her skin tight and tingly. She took a deep breath and shakily told herself that she would have to subdue reactions like that if she was to be offered the job of working with this man full-time. She might not like the guy but she couldn't afford to let that dislike control her responses.

'Yes,' she said, grateful that her voice was steady and cool.

'I'm going to read your CV and, provided I don't discover any…suggestion of little white lies in it, and provided your references check out, I'm going to offer you a full-time job working with me…'

'You *are*?'

'And I'm going to go the extra mile. After all, don't

preach what you can't practise. I'm going to open the door
for you to do that accountancy course you want to do.'

'Really?' A thousand jumbled thoughts were flying
through Alice's head but the one that was winning the
race was the one that was telling her that her life might
finally start moving forward, that she might finally have
enough money to start saving a little bit...

'And, naturally, you won't be called upon to sacrifice
your weekends unless imperative. In return...'

'You'll find that I'm up to anything you can throw at
me.'

'In that case...' He reached over for the telephone on her
desk and dialled a number then, before the line connected,
he said with a slow smile, 'You'll find that there are times
when you do need to involve yourself in my personal life,
Miss Morgan.' He handed her the phone. 'I won't be in
touch with this particular woman again, so maybe you can
set her straight on that score. And let's see whether you're
really up to anything I can throw at you...'

CHAPTER TWO

GABRIEL SAUNTERED INTO his office and closed the door behind him. He felt energised, pleased with his decision to hire the new woman on the spot. Normally, something as trivial as this would be left to his Personnel department but the impulse had felt right.

On the spur of the moment, he telephoned the company where she had last worked and spoke for five minutes to the boss, who gave her a glowing reference.

So, he had had an interminable string of relatively competent secretaries. They had all looked good, and why shouldn't he have gone for that? Some of them could even have been brought up to the standard he wanted had they not ended up becoming inconvenient. Lingering looks, offers to work as much overtime as he wanted, skirts that seemed to get shorter and tops more plunging as the days went on... All in all, pretty annoying in the end.

He wondered how this new one was dealing with the latest woman to have been dispatched from his life and he half-smiled when he imagined her tight disapproval.

Georgia had been exciting at the beginning. She had been enthusiastic and innovative in bed and, more importantly, had seemed to really take on board the ground rules for any relationship with him—namely, forget about looking for long-term commitment. So why had he got bored with her? She had certainly been eager to please and what man didn't want a woman willing to bend over backwards for him? He wondered whether there were just too many women willing to bend over backwards for him: gorgeous, sexy, voluptuous women whose vocabulary largely centred on the word 'yes'. In his high-octane, high-pressured life, the word 'yes' had always been a soothing counterpoint. Although of late...

He scrolled through the report in front of him and acknowledged another successful takeover that would allow him to expand certain aspects of one of his technology companies into Europe. In a rare moment of introspection, he grimly congratulated himself on the distance he had travelled from the foster-home kid with zero prospects to a man who ruled the world. He was sure he had felt more pleasure in the past when he had occasionally contemplated his achievements.

He had started on the trading floor, a sixteen-year-old gofer with an uncanny ability to read markets and predict trends. His first real kick had come when he had realised that the guys with the cut-glass accents and the country estates had begun to take him seriously when he spoke. They had started seeking him out and, with the instincts born of someone from the wrong side of the tracks who was hungry and ambitious, he had learnt how to ruthlessly use and eventually channel his talents. He had learnt when to share information and when to withhold it. He had learnt that money was power and power brought immunity from ever having to do what anyone else told him to do.

He became the man who gave the orders and he liked it that way. Thirty-two years old and he was untouchable.

The firm knock on the door snapped him out of his thoughts and he sat back in his chair and summoned her in.

This, Alice was thinking as she walked into his of-

fice, was why she could never like this guy. He had dialled a number and then left her to it and, from what she
had gleaned during that conversation with Georgia of the
husky voice, he was just the sort of inveterate playboy she
despised.

But the job was going to be hers and she wasn't going
to let this type of challenge kill her chances. He seemed
to have accepted her request for her weekends to remain
sacrosanct and had hired her without the usual bank of in-
terviews. She got the feeling that this was a departure for
him. So she could bend a little in this area...

Her face, however, was rigid with disapproval as she
sat in the chair indicated.

'I assume,' she began stiffly, 'that you would want to
see me to find out how my conversation went with your...
girlfriend...'

'Ex—ex-girlfriend. Hence the point of the conversation.
So that she could be left in no doubt as to where matters
stood.' The waves of disapproval emanating from her were
palpable. She looked as though she'd swallowed a lime and
was painfully having to digest it. 'I spoke to your ex-boss.
Sounds like a nice man. I'm thinking you were never required to step up to the plate and have any awkward conversations with his ex-lovers...'

Was he being deliberately provocative? The lazy intensity of his gaze and the suggestion of a smile on his lips
sent the blood rushing to her head and she tightened her
jacket around her and sat up a little straighter. Her crossed
legs felt as stiff as planks of wood, yet there was a curling
sensation low down in her pelvis that she chose to ignore.
Top of her mind right now was counting the ways she dis-
liked her new boss. Good-looking he might be...*stagger-
ingly good-looking*...but she decided on the spot that his
personality left her cold.

In a way, it would make for an excellent working relationship. She had already gleaned from her phone call with the unfortunate Georgia that the problem with his past few secretaries, apparently, had been with them all developing inappropriate crushes on him.

'I can't believe he's got one of his secretaries to do the dirty work for him!' Georgia had wailed down the line. 'Well, if you're like the other one...' she had sobbed, 'Showing off your boobs and thinking you can snap him up, then you're making a mistake! He's never going to go there! He doesn't like to mix work and play. He told me! So you can forget it!'

Georgia had lasted a mere two months, one week and three days. Was that the average duration of his relationships with women—a handful of months before he got bored and moved on to the next toy?

Thoughts that were usually deeply buried rose swiftly to the surface and she thought about her father—the years spent watching from the sidelines as he'd failed to return home, failed to pretend that he hadn't been playing away, failed to pay lip service to a marriage he'd wanted to ditch but couldn't afford to. She killed that pernicious, toxic trip down memory lane and dragged her wayward mind back to the present.

'Tom was and is a very happily married man,' Alice intoned. 'So, no, there were no awkward phone calls to women.' *And you should make your own phone calls,* she wanted to snap.

'I gather from your expression that I'm not winning a popularity contest at this moment in time?' Did he care one way or another? No. But if they were going to work together then there was no point in pretending to be a saint. Soon enough she would come into contact with the women who entered and left his life, barely producing a ripple.

She would have to get used to fending off the occasional uncomfortable phone call and, if her moral high ground didn't allow for that, then he needed to know right now.

'She was very upset,' Alice informed him, trying hard to avoid the trap of sounding judgemental, because what he got up to in his private life was none of her business. If he didn't care who he shared it with, then that was up to him.

And yet, she couldn't help feeling that there were sides to him that he shared with no one, and she couldn't quite work out what gave her that impression—something veiled in his eyes that belied the image of a man who laid all his cards on the table. He didn't give a damn whether she knew about his women or not but, yes, he *did* give a damn about other things, things she suspected he kept to himself.

Of course, it was fanciful thinking, because it didn't take a genius to work out that a man who had reached the meteoric heights that he had would not be the open, transparent type. He would be the type who revealed only what he wanted to and only when it served his purposes.

'I have no idea why,' Gabriel said wryly. 'I'd already informed her that I was pulling the plug on our relationship. Unfortunately, I think Georgia found it harder than she thought to accept the breakup.'

'Do you usually farm difficult conversations out to your secretaries?'

The edge of criticism in her voice should have got on his nerves but Gabriel found that it didn't. For once, he was in the company of a woman who seemed in no danger of developing a crush on him. Nor was she his type. He liked them small and curvy with an abundance of obvious charm. Prickly and challenging didn't work for him. Prickly and challenging smacked of an effort he had no enthusiasm for giving.

'I can't say the opportunity has arisen in the past few months,' Gabriel drawled.

And it wouldn't have happened now, Alice deduced, except for the fact that he had wanted to put her to the test. Maybe he thought that she would not be up to the task—too prim and proper. She didn't have to hear him say that to know that it was what he had been thinking and she bristled even though a part of her knew that, yes, she took life seriously. She had always had to. There had not been much scope to develop a frivolous side when she had spent so much of her youth supporting her mother through the innumerable bouts of her father's indiscretions.

Pamela Morgan had never seemed to have the strength to stand up to her bullying, philandering husband, so she had turned to Alice for moral support. By the time Rex Morgan had died, in a car accident, his wife had become a shadow of the girl who had married him in the false expectation of living happily ever after.

Alice's dreams had been put on hold and, when she looked back, she could see that she had spent her teenage years laying down the foundations for the person she would later become: reserved, cautious, lacking in the carefree gaiety that might have been her due, given a different set of circumstances.

Her one experience with the opposite sex had merely served to drive home to her that it never paid to think that anything good was a foregone conclusion.

'Is there anything else you'd like me to do now, and what time might I expect you to be in tomorrow morning? I don't know what your diary is.' The diary he never used.

'I keep my diary on my phone. I'll email you the contents. And tomorrow? I expect I'll be in…at my usual time. Then I'm away for the next three days. Think you can handle being on your own?'

'As I said, Mr Cabrera, I will do my utmost to deal with anything you can throw at me...'

Disgorged from the jumble of people on the tube three weeks later, it occurred to Alice that whatever had been thrown at her had obviously been full of all the right vitamins and proteins because she was enjoying her job. No, more than enjoying it. She got up early with a spring in her step, looking forward to the workload ahead of her and the slow creeping of responsibilities that were landing on her plate.

Her brain was being challenged in all sorts of ways. She was personally responsible for three large accounts. She had enrolled for her accountancy studies. And, by her standards, she was being paid a small fortune.

It was amazing, given the fact that she disapproved of much of what Gabriel stood for. She disapproved of his blatant womanising; she disapproved of the way he picked up lovers and then discarded them. He made no secret of the fact that he was as ruthless in his private life as he was in his working one. She disapproved of his supreme certainty that whatever he wanted would be his. She disapproved of the way every female employee, almost without exception, practically went down on bended knee whenever he deigned to address them. She disapproved of his ego.

On a daily basis, she fielded calls from women who wanted to talk to him and she could gauge from their hopeful, breathless voices that talking was not the only thing they wanted.

She disapproved of all of that.

The guy clearly didn't have to try when it came to the opposite sex, so he didn't. He was pursued and presumably, when he felt like it, he took one of his pursuers up on her offer and established something that couldn't even really be called a relationship.

He was lazy.

But so beautiful, a little voice in her head absently pointed out, and Alice halted for a second so that the crowds parted around her, some of them muttering impatiently under their breath.

She wouldn't deny that he had looks. The strong, aggressive lines of his lean, dark face were imprinted in her head with the force of a branding iron. She thought about him in passing more than she liked, then justified her lapses by telling herself that of course she would think of him—he was an exciting person to work for and she was only new to the job, hadn't had time to get used to him yet.

Which was why she knew just how long his dark lashes were and the way they could conceal the expression in his eyes... Which was how she knew that the second he entered the office, bringing all that force and vitality behind him, he would roll up the sleeves of his shirt, walk past her and immediately ask for his coffee.

She doubted that he even really noticed her. She was his über-efficient secretary who did as she was told faster than the speed of light. For long periods of time, he barely glanced in her direction at all.

She picked up speed, suddenly irritated for allowing her thoughts to stray down forbidden paths. He didn't notice her because she wasn't his type.

His type was...

No, she wasn't going to let her mind start speculating.

By now familiar with the impressive entrance foyer and well used to the hordes of workers and, later in the day, the tourists who were always milling about, Alice blanked everyone out as she strode purposefully towards the lift.

It was not yet eight. The three floors occupied by his

company would only be partly peopled. She liked the relative quiet as she was transported upwards…and upwards and upwards…

She felt a curl of excitement as she exited the lift. She barely recognised the emotion. Her head was full of what she had to do that day. The last thing she was expecting was to enter her office to the sight of two figures having an argument in Gabriel's office.

Through the slender panes of glass, Gabriel's face was dark with anger. She couldn't make out what was being said but his voice was low and deadly. The woman's, on the other hand…

She should interrupt. She should try to manage this situation because it was just the glorified version of what she occasionally had to do on the phone.

He didn't seem to care whether women chased him or not, or even whether they threw hissy fits down the end of the line, but he kept sharp dividing lines between work and play.

Obviously some poor woman had failed to pay attention to that dividing line and was paying the price.

And doesn't it serve him right?

The thought sprang from nowhere but, once it took hold, it couldn't be budged.

She had no idea who this woman was but why shouldn't he sort this situation out himself? Just because he had all the money and power in the world, it didn't mean that he could take the easy way out when it came to the situations he engendered with his women!

She calmly removed her lightweight coat and hung it up in the sliding cupboard. Then she made herself a cup of coffee and, with mug in hand, she sat at her desk and switched on her computer.

But she couldn't focus. Her eyes kept sliding from her

computer screen to the sketch being enacted behind Gabriel's closed door. That said, she was still shocked when the closed door was banged open and out flew a woman with waist-length dark hair and a porcelain-white complexion. Her red dress was skin-tight, her heels were five inches high at the very least and she was trailing a pink-and-black-checked summer coat over her shoulder.

She looked furious. Furious and upset. She paused just long enough to glare at Alice through tear-filled eyes.

'He's a pig!' She glared over her shoulder to where an impassive Gabriel was watching them both with steely-eyed coldness, then fixing enraged dark eyes on Alice. 'But at least he hasn't got one of those dolly birds working for him this time!'

'Georgia…' Gabriel's voice silenced what promised to be a tirade. He spoke very quietly and with such contained menace that Alice felt sorry for the poor woman. 'If you don't leave my premises immediately, I will call security and have you thrown out. And you…' He directed this at Alice who tilted her head to one side in perfect secretarial mode. 'Kindly escort Georgia out of the building and then come into my office…'

She was barely aware of Georgia talking non-stop on the way down in the lift. The diminutive brunette was angry, bitter and, reading between the lines, humiliated because she had never been dumped in her life before. Men chased *her* and *she* was the one responsible for doing any dumping.

Alice could have told her that she had taken on far more than she could ever have hoped to chew with a man like Gabriel.

'Well, at least you'll be safe as houses,' the other woman sniped as her parting shot. 'Gabriel would never look twice at someone like you. And tell him from me—I hope he rots in hell!'

The spurt of courage that had prompted her to stay put in her office twenty minutes earlier had evaporated by the time Alice returned there, having successfully deposited Georgia on the street outside. Still, there was no way that she intended to apologise for not having interrupted the scene in his office.

With any luck, he would simply brush over the whole incident and the day would commence as it always did, at full tilt.

'What the hell do you think you were playing at?' were his opening words as she walked into his office with her tablet in her hand, ready for the day to begin.

'I beg your pardon?' She started as he swooped round his desk to perch on the edge so that he was looming over her, face as dark as thunder.

'And don't give me that "butter wouldn't melt in your mouth" look! I saw the way you sneaked into the office and hid behind your computer!'

'I did not *sneak* into my office, Gabriel…' It always felt odd to call him by his Christian name but after three days of 'sir' and 'Mr Cabrera' and 'Mr Cabrera, sir' he had impatiently insisted that she drop the titles and call him Gabriel. It was one of those names that did not happily roll off the tongue. It was just too…*sexy*…

'Nor,' she asserted firmly, 'did I *hide* behind my computer!'

'You did both. You knew that I was trapped there with that woman and instead of offering to escort her out you ducked for cover and watched from the sidelines!'

'*That woman…?*'

Gabriel flushed darkly and raked long fingers through his hair. 'I'm not in the mood for your sermonising,' he growled, glaring at her.

'I didn't realise that I sermonised,' Alice said truthfully. She had her thoughts, but those she kept very much to herself.

'You don't have to! I know exactly what goes on in that head of yours whether you voice your opinions or not!'

Alice didn't say anything. His proximity was having a weird effect on her. If she looked directly at him, the glittering intensity of his dark eyes was unnerving. But if she looked a little lower, then she was confronted by his thigh, the taut pull of fine fabric over muscular legs, and that was even more unnerving. She could almost hear the steady drum roll of her heart and the rush of blood in her ears. He rarely invaded her space like this and she didn't have the resources to withstand the impact he had on her nervous system.

'Explain that remark.'

Alice had subtly pressed herself into the back of her chair. She wished he would let this conversation go because she could feel it teetering on the brink of getting too personal, and getting personal was something he had studiously avoided over the past three weeks. He never even asked her how she had spent her weekends.

'What remark?' she asked warily and he gave her another of those piercing looks that seemed to imply that he was perfectly aware that she was trying to dodge the conversation.

'You should try to avoid doing that as much as you can, you know,' he murmured softly.

It was like having her skin lightly brushed with a feather; the lazy speculation in his voice was even more disconcerting than the full-body impact of his towering presence so close to her.

'Aren't you going to ask me what I mean by that?' Gabriel continued into the lengthening silence, and Alice tried her best to dismiss the prickles of sensation racing through her body like tiny sparks of fire. 'No, of course you won't, but I'll tell you anyway. You should never try and wriggle away from a direct question. It makes me all the more determined to prise a suitable answer from you. The rule of thumb is that there's nothing more challenging to a man like me than a gauntlet that's been thrown down—and your silences count as gauntlets.' He didn't normally like challenges when it came to women but, hell, he liked *this* one...

A man like him?

Alice steeled herself to look him squarely in the face. 'I don't think it's very nice of you to throw your ex-lover out of the building because she happened to be upset with you.' There was a lot more she could have said on the subject but she chose to keep that to herself.

'It wasn't,' Gabriel grated, '*very nice* of my ex-lover to descend on me, in my office, so that she could throw a tantrum.' He vaulted upright and prowled through the office which she had somehow managed to make her own in the handful of weeks she had been working for him. There were two plants on the bookshelf, another on her desk and a discreet Buddha figurine which she kept next to the telephone. Having circled the room, he returned to stare down at her, hands thrust into his pockets.

'I don't suppose that was her intention,' Alice told him calmly. 'I don't think she came here planning to have a yelling fit at you. I think if she'd planned on screaming she could have done it down the telephone rather than come here and risk the humiliation of being ushered out of the building like a common criminal.'

'But then, if she'd used the telephone, she would have had to get past my faithful and extremely proficient secretary, wouldn't she?'

Alice blushed and wondered how two perfectly flattering adjectives could end up sounding so unappealing.

'Maybe,' he mused, leaning down, palms of his hands on her desk, 'she was overcome with a pressing need to vent. Do you think that might be it?'

Alice shrugged and for a few seconds their eyes tangled. Her mouth went dry and her brain seemed to seize up completely so that she had to suck in air and force herself to breathe evenly.

'Have *you* ever experienced that before, Alice?'

'Experienced what?' Alice asked in a hoarse whisper, and he laughed under his breath.

'The grip of passion that makes you behave irrationally...'

'I prefer to trust reasoning and logic,' she managed to say.

'So that's a *no*...'

'If you recall...' She was close to snapping because not only was he making her feel uncomfortable but he was enjoying himself. 'I *did* say to you when I took this job that I didn't want to talk about my private life!'

'Was that what we were doing? Talking about your private life?' He stood up, flexed his muscles, debated whether to let this conversation go and just as quickly decided not to. Georgia's untimely visit had dented his concentration and he was finding it strangely enjoyable to offload on his secretary. Offloading was not something he normally did. In his formidably controlled life, there was seldom any reason to, and he had to concede that, had Alice not been there, not been his secretary, he wouldn't have felt tempted.

But, hell, why deny it? She roused his curiosity. She was so contained, so secretive whilst giving the impression of being straightforward, so unwilling to share even the smallest of confidences, such as what she did on those precious weekends of hers that couldn't possibly be interrupted…

He would stake his fortune on 'nothing' and he wondered whether his curiosity was sparked by the mere fact that she never mentioned it. When you could have anything you wanted, including access to people's thoughts and emotions, what price for the person who withheld everything?

'You may think it's okay to treat women exactly how you like, but everyone has their story to tell, and you have no idea what sort of collateral damage you could be inflicting!' Her eyes skittered away from his narrowed gaze and she knew that she was beetroot-red and angry with him for encouraging an outburst that was inappropriate.

'Collateral damage…?' he asked thoughtfully.

'I apologise. I shouldn't have…said anything.' She offered him a weak smile which he chose to ignore.

'We work closely together,' he murmured. 'You should always feel free to speak your mind.'

'You like women speaking their minds, do you?' Alice asked tartly and was rewarded with one of those rare smiles that always knocked the breath out of her body.

'Touché… It can occasionally be a little tedious, but then I never encourage the women I date to ever think that it might be a good idea to give their thoughts an airing.'

Why not? Alice was tempted to ask. She didn't dare look at him because she had a sneaking suspicion that he might be able to read her mind.

Besides, didn't she know why? Why go to the bother of working at something meaningful if you could have whatever you wanted without putting the effort in? People got where they were because of circumstances shaping them over the course of time and, whatever the circumstances that had shaped Gabriel Cabrera, they had left him in a place where he just couldn't be bothered.

'What do you encourage them to do?' She asked her reluctant question, which was motivated by a burning curiosity she was desperate to kill whilst being unable to resist.

'I don't.' Gabriel gave her a slashing smile of satisfaction. 'And, now that we've plumbed the depths of my psyche, why don't we get down to doing something productive?'

It was nearly six by the time she surfaced. He had spent a good part of the day involved with high-level meetings, giving her the chance to quell the sludgy, disturbing feelings that had come to the fore during their conversation, when he had strayed beyond their normal boundaries like an invader testing a solid wall for cracks through which unwelcome entrance might be possible.

As she began clearing her desk to leave, she succumbed to a little smile at what an overactive imagination could produce. He didn't want to find out about *her*. He wasn't interested in whether there were cracks in her armour or not. He enjoyed pushing against barriers because that was the way he was built and, if the barriers happened to be around *her,* then push against them he would if the inclination took him.

As a woman, she held no interest for him.

She thought of Georgia of the husky voice and imagined that *that* was the sort of woman that interested him. Men always went for the same *type,* didn't they?

An image of Alan sprang uninvited into her head. Alan of the floppy blond hair and the brown eyes, who had ditched her for a version of womanhood not a million miles removed from her boss's ex. Flora was small and curvy as well. Not as stunning, and probably not as breezily self-confident about the power she had over the opposite sex, but, yes, fashioned from the same mould.

'You're smiling.'

She hadn't even been aware of Gabriel entering the office behind her as she shrugged on her jacket and she started and blushed.

'It's nearly the end of the week,' she responded automatically, although, thinking about it, her week days were more relaxing than her weekends, which were consumed with long trips down to visit her mother.

'Is working for me that much of a trial?' She had been awarded the same clothes allowance as the other employees on her level yet she still wore the same dreary suits to work. Black and shades of black seemed to be the preferred, professional option with his staff, yet her suits, although the requisite colour, didn't seem to fit with the same snug panache.

The errant thought occupied his mind for a few seconds and he frowned and pushed it away.

'Of course not. I...I love it, as a matter of fact.' He was lounging against the doorframe, as dramatically good-looking at the close of day as he was first thing in the morning. Where most people occasionally looked harried, he always seemed to be brimming over with vitality, however frantic his day might have been.

'That's good to hear because I haven't got around to having any kind of appraisal with you.'

Alice doubted he had ever done an appraisal in his life. If his employee didn't fit the bill, then he simply dispensed with them.

'Not,' he said, reading her mind with unnerving accuracy, 'that I make a habit of conducting appraisals of my secretaries.'

'Is that because they usually only last two minutes?'

A tingle of pure pleasure raced through her when he burst out laughing, which subsided eventually for him to cast appreciative eyes over her.

'Something like that,' he murmured. 'Seems a little pointless to give them an appraisal when they've already got one foot through the back door and their desk has been cleared.'

'Well…' He was blocking her way out and she dithered uncomfortably. Standing by him, it was brought home sharply just how tall he was. She was tall but he positively towered over her.

'Well, of course, you're on your way out. Is that what had you smiling?'

'I beg your pardon?'

'Your plans for the evening. Is that what put that smile on your face?'

If only you knew… If only you guessed that I was smiling at the notion that you would never look twice at me; smiling for being an idiot even to think about something like that.

His plans had been for the theatre, followed by dinner at one of the most exclusive restaurants in London.

The theatre, followed by dinner out—at a haunt for the paparazzi because the clientele was usually very high-profile—followed by…

Heat flooded her as she contemplated after-dinner sex with the man standing in front of her, still blocking her path. His hands on her body, his mouth exploring her, that dark, sexy voice whispering in her ear…

Her body jack-knifed into instant, crazy reaction. Liquid pooled between her legs and the unfamiliar tug of desire hit her like a ton of bricks, shocking in its intensity and as destabilising as the sudden onslaught of some ferocious disease. She couldn't move. Her legs were blocks of cement, nailing her to the floor as her imagination took flight in forbidden directions.

And, all the while, she could feel those dark, dark eyes pinned to her face.

'I have to go,' she said tightly. She went to push him aside and more heat flared inside her, making a mockery of her attempts to harness her prized composure.

He was a man she might respect but didn't like! A man whose brilliance she could admire whilst being left cold by his detachment!

Once out of the office, she fled…

CHAPTER THREE

ALICE WOKE WITH a start. In her dream, she had been running down an endlessly long corridor, chasing Gabriel who would occasionally glance over his shoulder, only to turn away and continue running. In the dream, she had no idea what lay at the end of that corridor, or even if there *was* an end to it, but she was filled with a sense of terrifying foreboding, wanting to stop and yet propelled forward by some power greater than her own.

She was slick with perspiration and completely disoriented and it took her a few seconds to realise that her mobile was ringing. Not the sharp, insistent buzz of her alarm but actually ringing.

'Good. You're awake.'

Hard on the heels of her disturbing dream, Gabriel's voice cut through the fog of her sleepiness as effectively as a bucket of ice-cold water, and she sat up in bed, glancing at the clock on her bedside table which showed that it wasn't yet six-thirty.

'Is that you, Gabriel?'

'How many calls do you get from men at this hour of the morning? No, don't answer that.'

'What's wrong with your voice?' This was the first time he had ever called her at home on her mobile and she looked around her furtively, as though suspecting that at any second he might materialise from the shadows.

Thankfully, her bedroom was as it always was—small with magnolia walls, some nondescript curtains and two colourful pictures on either side of the dressing table, scenes of Cornwall painted by a local artist whom Alice knew vaguely through her mother. An averagely passable room in a small, uninteresting house whose only selling point was its proximity to the tube.

In the bedroom next to hers, her flat mate, Lucy, would still be sleeping.

'It seems I'm ill.'

'You're *ill*?' The thought of Gabriel being ill was almost inconceivable and she felt a sudden grip of panic.

Whatever was wrong with him, it would be serious. He was not the sort of man to succumb to a passing virus. He was just too...*strong*. She couldn't imagine that there could be any virus on the planet daring enough to attack him.

'Ill with *what*?' She brought the decibel level of her worried voice down to normal. 'Have you called the doctor?'

'Of course not.'

'What do you mean *of course not*?'

'Are you dressed?'

His impatient voice, which she had become accustomed to, sliced through her concern and she glanced in the dressing-table mirror facing her to see her still sleepy face staring back at her.

Her straight hair was all over the place and the baggy tee-shirt, her bedtime attire of choice, was half-slipping off her shoulder, exposing the soft swell of a breast.

Self-consciously, she hoiked it up and then lay back against the pillow.

'Gabriel, my alarm doesn't go off for another forty-five minutes...'

'In that case, switch it off and think about getting up and out of bed.'

'What's wrong?'

'Sore throat. Headache. High fever. I've got flu.'

'You've phoned me at…at *six-twenty* in the morning to tell me that you've *got a cold*?'

'I think you'll find that what I have is considerably more serious than *a cold*. You need to get up, get into the office and bring the two files I left on my desk. Not all of the information is on my computer and I need to access it in its entirety.'

She had worked with him long enough to know that he dished out orders in the full expectation that they would not be countermanded, but she was still outraged that he had seen fit to yank her out of sleep so that he could…

What, exactly?

'Bring your files?'

'Correct. To my house. And bring your computer as well. You'll have to work from here. It's not ideal but it's the best I can come up with. I can't make it into the office today.'

'Surely you can just take the day off if you're not feeling well, Gabriel?' *Like any other normal human being,* she was tempted to add. 'If you tell me what you want me to work on, I can do it in the office and I can scan and email the files over to you, if you really think that you're up to working.'

'If I'd wanted you to do that, I would have said so. And I can't keep talking indefinitely. My throat's infected. If you head for the office now, you can be with me within an hour and a half. Less, if you get your skates on. Got a pen?'

'A pen?' Alice parroted in dismay as this new unfolding of her day ahead began to take shape in her head.

'A pen—instrument for writing. Have you got one to hand? You'll need to write down my address and postcode. And for God's sake, take a taxi, Alice. I know you're fond of the London public transport system, but we might as well get this show on the road as quickly as possible. There's a lot to get through and I won't be up to much beyond six… It's ridiculous. I haven't been ill in years. I must have caught this from you.'

'You haven't caught anything from me! I'm fighting fit!'

'Good. Because you have a lot to get through today. Now, let me give you my address.'

She got a pen and wrote down his address and then listened as he rattled off a few more orders and then… dial tone.

She had no time for breakfast. She could have grabbed something but for some unaccountable reason she found herself rushing to have a shower, rushing to get dressed, rushing to head for the tube and then, on the spur of the moment, hailing a black cab—because she could almost feel those dark eyes peering at her from wherever he was.

The man was utterly impossible. He really and truly didn't care what discomfort he caused for other people. He took it as his God given right to disrupt other people's plans and then excused himself his own arrogance by giving one of those elegant shrugs and waving aside all objections because, after all, comparatively he paid them the earth. He was brilliant, he did as he pleased, and why on earth would anyone not want to fall in line?

She made it to his house within the hour and only when the taxi had deposited her there did her nervous system kick back into gear.

This was unknown territory. Had anyone in the office ever been to his house? Company entertaining was all done in restaurants, or expensive venues in the City, and he certainly wasn't the avuncular sort of boss who hosted little parties so that his employees could bond with one another.

She stared at the impressive Georgian facade and hesitated. What had she expected? She didn't know. Something far less grand—a penthouse apartment, perhaps. There was, after all, only *one* of him, even if he had all the money in the world to play with. Why did he need a London mansion?

Black brass railings cordoned off the house and matched all the other black brass railings of the mansions alongside it. Standing here, gazing up with her little handbag, her company case full of files and her computer, she felt as though she might be arrested at any moment for the crime of just not quite blending in.

Inhaling deeply, she rang the buzzer and his disconnected voice came on the line.

'I'll buzz you in. You'll find me upstairs.'

'Where...?' But the door had popped open; as to his whereabouts...she assumed she would have to locate him through sheer guesswork.

Her heart was beating madly as she stared around her. The hall was absolutely enormous, almost as big as the entire ground floor of her shared house. Victorian tiles were broken by a pale Persian rug and ahead of her a staircase wound its elegant way upwards.

What was he doing upstairs? Was his office there?

She smoothed down her skirt with perspiring hands. She could have worn something more casual— could have worn her jeans and a tee-shirt, considering she wouldn't actually be in the office—but she hadn't. She had dressed as she always did, in a neat black skirt, her white short-sleeved blouse and her little black jacket. She was very glad she had gone for the formal option.

It was harder to locate him than she would have thought possible because the house was huge, split into three storeys with myriad rooms to the left and right of the staircase. She peered into two sitting rooms and several bedrooms before she eventually hit the right one at the very end of the wide corridor.

Through the half-open door, she glimpsed rumpled covers on a bed and she hesitantly knocked.

'About time! How long does it take one person to make her way through a house?'

Gabriel was propped up in bed. The rumpled duvet had been shoved to one side and he was in a black dressing gown, legs bare, sliver of chest exposed, black hair tousled. Next to him was his computer, on which he had clearly been working.

Alice averted her eyes and felt a tightening in her chest, almost as if she was in the grip of an incipient panic attack.

'Are we going to be…er…working *here*?'

'Stop hovering by the door and come inside. And where else do you suggest we hold proceedings?'

'I passed an office…'

'I can't get out of bed. I'm ill.' This was the first time in living memory that he had been in his bed and the woman standing in his bedroom looked as though the last thing she wanted was to be there. 'And, as you can see, this isn't a bedroom. It's a suite.' He nodded to the sofa which was by the tall windows and the long coffee table in front of it. 'Does it make you uncomfortable, Alice?'

'Of course not.' But there was a wicked gleam in his eyes which *did* make her uncomfortable. Gabriel would not be happy with being bed-ridden for whatever reason. He was not the sort of man whose restless energy could be contained without it emerging somewhere else. The Devil worked on idle hands and for him his hands would be idle…

'I just think that it might be more suitable if we were in an office environment.'

'Why? Everything I need is right here. Where are the

files? And for God's sake, sit down! How are you going to work if you keep standing by the door?'

He shifted impatiently and Alice gulped as yet more of that hard, bronzed torso was revealed.

He should be in his suit. He should be properly attired. There was an intimacy here that had her nerves all over the place and she was so keen to make sure that he didn't see that, her movements were stiff and awkward, her mouth more tightly pursed, her hands white as they gripped the case she had brought with her.

She felt horrendously uncomfortable in her knee-length black skirt, and her sheer black tights were itchy against her legs.

'Have you...taken anything for your cold?' she asked as she sat gingerly on the sofa and tried not to look at him without actually looking away; tried to mentally blank him out, which was next to impossible. 'Sorry, I meant *flu*?'

'Of course not.'

'Why ever not?'

'What good would that do? The thing just has to run its course.'

'I'll get you some paracetamol.'

'You will sit and start going through the Dickson file with me.'

'Where is your medicine cabinet?'

'I don't have one.'

Alice shot him an exasperated look and walked across to stand over him with her arms folded. 'You look terrible.'

'Good. You're waking up to the fact that I'm seriously ill.'

'And you look terrible because you're refusing to help yourself. You are *not* seriously ill, Gabriel. You have a spring cold. You're just not accustomed to being under the weather.'

'What do you mean, I'm *refusing to help myself*?' Gabriel growled. 'You're a woman! Where's your milk of human kindness? Do you know how many women would kill to be in this position—to be able to prove that they're domestic goddesses by cooking me something to eat and playing at Florence Nightingale!'

'In which case...' She handed him his mobile phone. 'Please feel free to call any one of them. I'm more than happy to be replaced.'

'Sit down!' he roared, before spluttering into a coughing fit which Alice observed without budging, arms still folded, cool as a cucumber and grudgingly amused at seeing her all-powerful boss losing his control because he was in the grip of nothing more serious than a simple passing cold.

He could be vulnerable. In a way least expected, he was showing her that he could be petulant, utterly exasperating in a very human way and...

Stupidly endearing with it.

'I have some tablets in my handbag. I'll fetch you a glass of water and you're going to take them. They might not cure your cold but they'll relieve your symptoms.'

'Does that include my roasting fever? I'm burning up. Feel me if you don't believe me.'

Alice sighed and felt his forehead and, as she did so, she felt a throbbing ache rip through her, scattering her self-composure for a second or two.

'You have a slight temperature.' She yanked her hand back and surreptitiously wiped it on her skirt, hoping to rid herself of the spark that had flared between them, dangerously, electrifyingly alive and as threatening as her dream had been to her peace of mind.

Why the sudden *awareness* of the man? she wondered. She disapproved of him as much now as she had done when she had first met him. So, they worked well together. So, maybe there were different sides to him; he wasn't the one-dimensional guy she had chosen to categorise him as...

But why was it that the minute he was within touching distance of her she became as jumpy as a cat on a hot tin roof?

It was galling to think that she might have fallen into the same pathetic trap as all his other secretaries and she instantly killed that notion by telling herself that she hadn't. He was fabulously good-looking and she was only human, after all. What reaction he evoked was one she could squash without any difficulty.

Although right now, having to sit in the same room as him when he was, quite frankly, indecently under-dressed...

She strode out of the room into the adjacent *en suite* bathroom, ignoring the slightly damp white towel care-lessly slung on the heated towel rail, and emerged with a glass of tap water and the tablets which she had extracted from her bag.

'Take them.'

'You're extremely bossy.' But he took the tablets from her and swallowed them with a gulp of water. 'Not a fem-inine trait.'

Alice blushed, hot, flustered and irritated. 'I'm not here to be "feminine",' she retorted tartly. 'I'm here to go through some files which couldn't possibly wait until next week. You have your string of girlfriends to distract you with their feminine wiles.'

'I'm a girlfriend-free zone at the moment, as it happens. Although I'm sure you're already aware of that, consider-ing you're the one who's responsible for booking the ven-ues I go to with them.'

The unfeminine, drab-but-efficient secretary who an-

swers to your beck and call and books all the exciting places you take your women to...

So far, she had just booked the opera, but he was still fresh out of his relationship with Georgia and perhaps not quite there when it came to diving into a brand new relationship with another woman. The opera for two...

'What happened to your opera companion?' She allowed herself to be distracted, swept away on the disagreeable thought that life was passing her by as she stood on the sidelines, somehow waiting for it to happen.

She had never felt this way before. She had been happy to settle into a routine and to accept that, if things hadn't turned out the way she had planned, then they could be worse. This was her lot and so be it.

Was it Gabriel's overwhelming vitality that made her feel slow and sluggish in comparison? Was it the fact that she was the dullard behind the computer who booked the exciting events for exciting women?

'Turns out she didn't have what it takes. Admittedly, she was sexy as hell,' he mused lazily. 'But sadly the legs, the curves, the winning pout...weren't enough to save her from being interminably boring.'

Alice's rictus smile felt strained at the edges. *Another one bites the dust*, she thought with simmering resentment. Time to move on to another model and, fingers crossed, the legs, the curves and yet another winning pout might be combined with half a personality. While other *normal* people stuck things out because life was just not one long array of delectable dishes to be sampled and discarded, the Man Who Had It All just couldn't be bothered with little niceties like that.

'Maybe,' he continued in the same musing, sexy voice, 'I should incorporate that into your job description... Maybe I should delegate you to finding me someone who won't prove tiresome after five seconds. Think you can handle it?'

Anger replaced resentment and, suddenly, Alice saw red. Who the heck did he think she was? Some kind of facilitator to ensure that even less effort was required by him when it came to finding a woman? Did he have any idea how condescending he sounded? How terminally *dull* he made her feel? Did he even *care*?

'You…you…you have to be the *laziest man* I have ever met in my *entire life*!'

'Come again?'

'You heard me, Gabriel. You're lazy!' Hot, angry eyes raked over that sexy, prone body with the silk dressing gown allowing her far too wide-ranging a view of hard muscle and sinew. 'You may work like the Devil, and you may have the Midas touch, but you can't even be bothered to sort your own emotional life out! Why don't you put some thought into booking the stuff you decide to do with your women? Why don't you field your own calls and make your own excuses when you don't want to see someone? You even got me to *choose* a parting gift for Georgia after she stormed out of your office! Something conciliatory, you said, money no object—and you never even bothered to find out *what* I'd chosen! How lazy is that?'

She had picked out a huge bouquet of flowers and a designer scarf in the colours of the coat the other woman had been wearing when she had had her hissy fit in his office. It had been eye-wateringly expensive but she doubted he would even raise an eyebrow when it showed up on his statement.

'You're going beyond your brief,' Gabriel told her coolly. *Lazy? Him? Hell, he worked all the hours God made! He had climbed the ladder no one thought he could and he had climbed it to the very top and built a castle there!*

But she hadn't been referring to his unparalleled success on the work front, had she? She had gone straight to
the emotional side of his life. Typical of a woman, he told
himself without the slightest inclination to analyse what
she had said. As far as he was concerned, he had come
from nothing and now had everything. He could have any
woman he wanted. They flocked to him and he was astute
enough to suspect that his sizeable bank balance had a lot
to do with it. Would they still have flocked in their droves
if he had never climbed that ladder? If the foster-care kid
had become the welfare-dependent adult? Somehow, he
didn't think so.

No, the only thing he could rely upon was his ability
to make money and to use his wealth to buy himself absolute freedom. Everything else fell by the wayside in
comparison.

But the description still left a sour taste in his mouth.

'I'm sorry,' Alice told him without hesitation. 'I didn't
mean to be critical.'

Gabriel could have taken her up on that insincere asser-
tion. He didn't. Instead, he turned to the reason she was
there in the first place and the next three hours were spent
poring over the files she had brought with her.

She had a good brain. She had creative and different
ways of looking at potential problems. She could quickly
do the maths when it came to sounding out the viability
of certain tricky areas.

She had obviously forgotten her outburst but he still
caught himself staring at her every so often, her down-bent
head, her slender fingers tapping expertly on the keyboard
as she amended documents.

And the damn woman had been right about the tablets.
By midday, he was feeling better.

'Right.' He swung his legs over the side of the bed and

Alice, ensconced on the sofa by the window, looked at him in alarm.

'What are you doing?' She had just about forgotten that she was working with him in his bedroom and that he was wearing nothing but a flimsy black robe which he was at no pains to pull tightly around him. She had told her wayward eyes to get a grip and thankfully, under the onslaught of work, they had. She had established their routine of sorts. And now he was standing up and tying the belt of the bathrobe only after she had glimpsed boxer shorts and brown thighs speckled with fine dark hair. He had amazing ankles. She kept her eyes firmly riveted on that fairly harmless section of his body as he strolled towards the bathroom and informed her that he was going to have a shower.

'Why don't you wait for me in the kitchen? We can grab something to eat before we carry on.'

'You seem a lot better,' Alice ventured. 'Are you sure you wouldn't rather wrap up what we've been doing and really…um…harness your energies? They say that the best way to get rid of a cold—sorry, flu—is to just take it easy and rest.'

'That might work for some people but not for me. Taking it easy isn't my style. Now, unless you want to follow me into the bathroom so that we can continue discussing the situation with the electronics subsidiary, I suggest you stretch your legs and head downstairs. In fact…' He paused by the door and looked at her, his eyes showing just the merest flicker of amusement even though his tone of voice remained bland. 'You could always make yourself useful and cook us something to eat. You'll find the fridge and the cupboards well-stocked. In keeping with my laziness, I have someone who makes sure that they are…'

With which he disappeared into the bathroom, not bothering to lock the door, leaving her with the frustrated feeling that somehow the rug had been neatly pulled out from under her feet.

Since when did her secretarial duties encompass cooking for the boss? Did the man know how to do anything but take advantage? Since when had it been written into her contract that she would have to fly over to his house, faster than the speed of light, so that she could plough through endless files with him because he happened to have caught a passing bug?

And why on earth hadn't she objected more than she had? Why on earth did she feel so *alive* even when she was around him?

Downstairs, she looked around a kitchen where everything, from granite counters to gadgets, was polished to a high shine. She guessed that the person responsible for making sure that the fridge and cupboards were stocked with food was also responsible for making sure that dust and dirt didn't find a foothold.

There was bread, ham, eggs and all manner of delicacies in the fridge and, after several attempts, she located the whereabouts of the tea, various kinds, and also various kinds of coffee.

'I could always order in…' His voice drawled behind her and Alice spun round, skin burning as though she had been caught red-handed with her hand in the till.

Gabriel wandered towards her, freshly showered and thankfully out of his bathrobe and in clothes—although his clothes were no less disconcerting, because he was in a pair of black jeans and a baggy rugby shirt. She couldn't expect him to get dressed in his usual suit to stay home, but she wished that he had, because it would have cemented the boss-secretary line between them, would have reinforced their respective roles.

He was the essence of the alpha male—tall, dominant, with the sleek, latent power of a predator. In fact, there were times when she felt distinctly like prey when she was around him. This was one of those times, although she didn't know why. She just knew that watching him pad through the kitchen barefoot, in jeans that delineated every powerful line of his body, was horribly unsettling.

'You should be wearing something on your feet,' she said inanely as he joined her by the kitchen counter so that he could help with the tea making. 'You might be feeling better thanks to the tablets, but you don't want to get a relapse.'

'Underfloor heating in the kitchen. If you'd take those black pumps off, you'd find that the floor is very warm.' She hadn't so much as undone the top button of her very neat white shirt, he thought. She was out of the office, and there had been no need to wear office garb, but predictably she had not deviated from her strict dress code. She hadn't even kicked off her sensible patent shoes for the entire time she had been sitting on the sofa in his bedroom taking notes and amending reports on her computer.

She was the stiffest, least relaxed woman he had ever met. Yet, when she had exploded, he had glimpsed a side to her that was as volatile and as fiery as a volcano. It made sense. She was smart, she had a good brain. That in itself would indicate that there was more to her than the dutiful secretary who spoke her mind, but politely, and always managed to leave the impression that there was a lot more to her than met the eye.

He wondered *what*.

Having grown accustomed to a diet of very willing and very beautiful women, he let his mind wander over the very prickly, very proper and very average Miss Alice

Morgan. And, once there, his mind showed every inclination of staying put.

Her dress code was so damned bland that it positively encouraged the eye to look away with boredom, but there was a pale delicacy to her face and a fullness to her mouth that hinted at a sensuality he suspected she was not aware of.

And just like that he felt himself harden.

'I would rather finish what we're doing and then head home.' Alice was uncomfortable with this domestic game they seemed to be playing. She hadn't signed up for this and she didn't know how to deal with being yanked out of her comfort zone.

Gabriel scowled. Without warning, he imagined her taking it between those cool hands of hers, lowering her mouth to it and licking it with her very delicate pink tongue. The graphic clarity of the image shocked him.

'Too bad,' he snapped. 'You're not being paid to skive off early just because I'm not fighting fit.'

What had brought *that* on? Alice wondered. Maybe he was getting to the end of his tether being cooped up in his house with a woman who wasn't his temporary bed partner. He was probably used to sharing his kitchen with a Georgia lookalike, except one in even less clothing. A Georgia lookalike wearing nothing but an apron and waving a spatula about with a come-hither grin.

'That's not fair,' she told him quietly. 'I'm just not very hungry; please don't think that you have to break off because of me.'

'I'm not,' Gabriel said shortly. He was still aching, his erection still hard and throbbing, and his imagination was still galloping merrily on a free rein. Without a trace of vanity, he knew that most women would kill to be in her position—in his kitchen with him, cooking. He had yet to allow any woman to cook for him. Why give them the wrong ideas? No, he entertained them in the relative safety of expensive restaurants. That way they couldn't start harbouring unrealistic ideas of domesticating him.

Yet here she was, standing with her back pressed against his kitchen counter, trying to find excuses to leave.

It was ludicrous to let that get under his skin but, coming hard on the heels of the erotic thoughts that had taken root in his head, it did.

He fished his mobile phone out of his pocket, called his friend and head chef at one of the top restaurants in the city and ordered a meal for two, menu unspecified. As he spoke, he kept his eyes pinned to Alice's face and she angrily wondered whether this was an attempt to generate some sort of guilt complex in her because she hadn't jumped at the chance of cooking a meal for him.

The more she thought about Gabriel, the more she realised just how lazy he was in his personal life. But, if he thought that he could make inroads into *her,* somehow turn her into one of his followers who did every single thing he wanted with a smile on their face, then he was in for a shock.

'You do realise that there's still a hell of a lot of work to do on Trans-Telecom,' he grated, sitting on one of the chrome and leather chairs by the kitchen table. He could feel the temperature he had managed to keep at bay with the tablets begin to rise as the pain killers wore off. 'You don't have to stand over there!' he snapped. 'If you're going to catch anything from me, then chances are you will have caught it already!'

'I thought you had covered most of the technical details on that.' Alice walked towards him and perched facing him. The thought that he might be infectious hadn't even crossed her mind. She had been far too busy just fretting about being in his house with him! He obviously hadn't shaved this morning and the darkening of stubble on his face was sinfully, extravagantly attractive.

'There's a deadline on this deal. The lawyers have pored over it with a fine-tooth comb but I still need to make sure that all bases are covered. I can't afford to have a comma in the wrong place or else there's the chance the whole thing will be called off. It's taken long enough for me to get the family on board with the concept of selling. I don't want any delay to have them getting cold feet at the last minute.'

Alice nodded. She was mesmerised by the intensity of his eyes, the perfect command he had when he was in work mode; the sheer, unadulterated sexiness of him in casual clothes. When it came to business, he was a machine. He could focus for hours on end without losing concentration. He could tackle a problem at eight in the morning and not let up until he had solved it, whether it took him two minutes, two hours or two days. She watched his hands as he gestured, her brow creased in a small frown which she hoped would convey a suitable level of concentration.

'And I'm afraid you have no choice in the matter…'

Alice started as she caught the tail end of his sentence.

'Have you been listening to a word I've been saying, Alice?' Just at that point, the doorbell rang and he returned a minute or two later with two bags filled with beautifully packed gourmet food.

'I'm sorry. Of course. You were talking about Trans-Telecom…'

'And informing you that you might get away with avoiding work duty this weekend but I'm giving you advance warning from now that, whatever plans you have for next weekend, you're going to have to cancel because you're coming to Paris with me to sign off on this deal. I'll need you there to transcribe everything that's said and agreed, word for word.'

'Next weekend…'

'Next weekend. So you can spend next week getting your head round it.'

Of course her mother would be fine for one weekend. Alice knew that but she still felt a stab of guilt. She knew that she could have just told him what her weekend plans were, confided the situation about her mother with him, but somehow that would have felt like another line being crossed and she didn't want to cross any more of those lines.

Besides, Gabriel Cabrera was many things, but a warm and fluffy person who encouraged girlish confidences was not one of those things.

Nor was she the fluffy, girlish type to dispense them.

'Of course,' she said brightly. 'I'll make sure that I… rearrange my weekend plans…'

Which were what, exactly? Gabriel wondered.

'Good. In that case, twenty minutes to eat, and then let's carry on…'

CHAPTER FOUR

ALICE HAD NOT been out of the country on a holiday for a while. She knew that this wasn't going to be a holiday—the opposite. But she would still be leaving the country and how hard would it be to take a little time out and explore some of the city on her own? Even if it meant grabbing an hour or two when they weren't entertaining clients or working.

And her mother had taken it well—better than Alice had expected, in fact.

She had been down in Devon, as usual, at the weekend and had decided, before she had even stepped foot in her mother's little two-bedroom cottage in the village, that she would break the news when she was about to leave.

Pamela Morgan lived on her nerves. A highly strung woman even in the very best of times, she had become progressively more neurotic and mentally fragile during the long course of her broken marriage.

Still only in her mid-fifties, she remained a beautiful woman, beautiful in a way Alice knew she never could be. Her mother was small, blonde, with a faraway look in her big blue eyes. She was the ultimate helpless damsel that men seemed to adore.

But that ridiculous beauty had been as much of a burden in the long run as it had been a blessing. Growing up,

Alice had watched helplessly from the sidelines as her mother had floundered under the crushing weight of her husband's arrogant, far more flamboyant personality. She hadn't seemed to possess the strength to break free. She was the classic example of a woman who had always relied on her looks and, when the going had got tough, had had nothing else upon which to fall back.

When Rex Morgan had begun to lose interest in his pretty wife, she had not been able to cope. She had desperately tried to make herself prettier—had done her hair in a thousand different styles, dyed it in a hundred different shades of vanilla blonde, had dieted until her figure made men stop in their tracks—but none of it had ever been enough. In the end she had given up, choosing instead to remain passive as her husband's philandering had beome more and more outrageous.

She had cowered when he had bellowed and waited without complaining when he had disappeared for days on end, reappearing without a word of explanation but reeking of perfume.

She had sat quietly and in fear as he had sapped every ounce of her confidence so that she could no longer see a way out, far less find the courage to look for it. And she had not complained when he had told her that, if it weren't for the money, he would have walked out on the marriage a long time ago.

The fact was that he'd been financially tied to her. There was still a mortgage on the house, too many bills to pay, and if they divorced and she got her fair share he would have ended up living in something ugly and nasty, no longer able to live it up with his various women.

So he had stayed put but he had made sure to make life as unpleasant for his fragile wife as he could.

Whenever Alice felt a little insecure about the way

she looked, she would sternly tell herself that good looks brought heartache. Look at her mother.

And look at those girls Gabriel dated, the Georgia look-alikes. Who said that a woman with beauty had it all?

Rex Morgan was dead now, in a car accident that had released his wife from her captivity, but he had left a telling legacy behind him. Pamela Morgan was housebound and had been for a while. The thought of leaving the four walls around her and venturing outside terrified her. Over time, and in small but significant stages, she had gradually become agoraphobic and was fortunate now to live in a small village where people looked in on her during the week to make sure that she was okay. In a city, where their house had been, she would have been completely lost.

At weekends, Alice would gently try to ease her out into the garden and, a couple of times recently, actually down to the nearest shop, although that had been a lengthy exercise.

She paid for professional help, which cost an arm and a leg, but recovery was tortoise-slow and uncertain.

Weekends, Alice suspected, were her mother's favourite times, so Alice made sure to reserve those weekends for her, whatever the personal cost.

And, after a year and a half of treatment and regular weekend visits, Alice felt like she was beginning to see a slightly different woman in her mother. She seemed less tentative, more open to a short walk. Of course, the treatment would continue. In conjunction with the occasional pep talk, Alice felt confident that at some point in time she would be able to have more than just the odd weekend away from her mother's side.

To do what, she had no idea. Her love life post-Alan was non-existent and, whenever her mother gently asked her about that, she was always quick to point out that she didn't need a guy.

The unspoken message was: *why would I? Just look at Dad...look at Alan... Men are trouble...*

She had told her mother bits and pieces about Gabriel as well, which cemented that unspoken message.

But things seemed to be progressing and so, when Alice had sat her down and told her that she wouldn't be able to make it the following weekend because of work, she was pleasantly surprised by her mother's reaction.

'That's absolutely fine,' Pamela had said with a smile. 'I need to know how to be a little more independent.'

Which, Alice thought, meant that the very costly professional whose services she was paying for was actually beginning to make a difference.

So, yes, she was looking forward to Paris.

They had spent the past week working flat out on every single aspect of the deal that could go wrong. In between, there had been the usual high-volume work load. She had been rushed off her feet and had enjoyed every minute of it.

And Gabriel's so-called flu had disappeared as quickly as it had come, although he hadn't failed to remind her that she was probably the one who had given it to him, which had made her lips twitch with amusement.

They had arranged to meet at the airport and now, waiting for her taxi to arrive, Alice once again ticked off the mental checklist in her head.

All necessary work documents, including her work laptop, would be in hand luggage. She had her mobile phone and all the necessary work clothes packed.

They would be going for four days and she had managed to fit everything into one average-sized suitcase with room to spare.

Outside, the weather was cool but sunny, and she gave in to a heady feeling of complete freedom. The feeling was so unusual that for a second or two she felt a painful pang that this was something she should have more of; that this was something most girls her age would take absolutely for granted and yet here she was, savouring it like a tasty morsel that would vanish all too soon.

Tasty morsel! She would be in the company of Gabriel most of the time!

Like a runaway train, her mind zoomed off at speed to the memory of him in his bathrobe—the sight of that bare chest, those strong, muscled legs, the way he had been prone on his king-sized bed, macho, dominant and oozing raw sex appeal.

She uneasily shoved aside the unacceptable thought that part of her excitement might have to do with just being with him for four uninterrupted days in Paris, of all places.

Her phoned beeped with the taxi announcing itself outside and, ready for the short trip to Heathrow, Alice focused on practical issues.

Her mother was fine. She hadn't forgotten anything. Another big deal was brewing on the sidelines and she had thought to read up on the company in question and download relevant facts that Gabriel might find useful.

She made it to the airport to find Gabriel already there and waiting at the designated spot by the first-class check-in counter.

He eyed her case sceptically.

'Is that all the luggage you've brought with you?' Annoyingly, she had been on his mind more than usual. He didn't know what he expected when she joined him at the airport but, unsurprisingly, she was in her usual work uniform of nondescript grey suit, a lighter one to accommodate the milder weather, and her neat black patent leather pumps.

'We'll only be gone for four days.' Alice's eyes skirted around him. He was elegantly casual in some cream trousers and a cream jumper under which he was wearing a striped shirt. He looked expensive, sophisticated and drop-dead gorgeous, the sort of man who wouldn't be travelling anything other than first class.

'I've dated women who have packed more than you have for an overnight stay in a hotel,' Gabriel remarked drily. He was discovering that he enjoyed the way she blushed, enjoyed the way her eyes never quite met his whenever she felt that something he said might have been a little too provocative.

He checked her in, holding up her passport so that he could examine the unflattering picture of her, and then they headed to the first-class lounge.

Excitement rippled through her.

'I've never been to Paris,' she confided, impressed with the first-class lounge with its comfortable seating, waiter service and upmarket lounge-bar feel.

Gabriel tilted his head to one side, pleasantly surprised, because she so rarely said anything to him of a personal nature.

In any other woman, that would have been a definite plus point. In her, he found it weirdly irritating. It was as if the more she failed to tell him, the more he wanted to find out.

'Never?'

'Never.'

'I thought school trips over here always involved at least one compulsory trip to France…or have you been to other bits of France?'

Alice thought of her school days. The state school she had attended hadn't been great and she had had next to no supervision at home. Her father had been absent most of the time, either physically or mentally, and her mother had increasingly removed herself from the normal day to day things that most mothers did, burrowing down in her own misery.

'I went to Spain once.' She detoured around his direct question. 'One of my school friends asked me over with her for two weeks over summer when I was fourteen. It was the nicest holiday I can remember having.'

'What about family holidays?'

'There weren't many of those,' Alice said abruptly.

'I know the feeling.'

She looked at him, startled. She knew next to nothing about his past. He came to her as the man already formed, the billionaire with no emotional ties and no desire to form any. He was the brilliant, talented, driven guy who worked hard and played hard; who snapped his fingers and expected the world to jump, but who rarely seemed to put himself out for anyone.

She teetered on the brink of asking him for details. Curiosity clamped its teeth into her but for some reason the thought of stepping over that brink terrified her and she changed the subject, asking him about the places he had been and the countries he had visited.

Besides, would he even share personal details with her? He was intensely private and guarded in what he revealed.

Gabriel noted the way she had backed away from following up on his remark. He wasn't too sure why he had said that in the first place. He had never felt inclined to let any woman into his past. Would he have told her about his foster-home background? Doubtful, although in fairness he couldn't imagine her exclaiming with false sympathy or using it as leverage to try to prise him open like a shell.

His interest spiked and he looked at her with cool, guarded eyes.

The four-day trip to Paris suddenly seemed ripe with all sorts of possibilities. He wondered whether she had ever let her hair down, gone wild, got drunk, danced on tables. He couldn't see it. He wondered what she was thinking, what was going through her head.

What she did on those weekends.

He caught himself wondering whether there was a man in her life, despite protests to the contrary...

The questions settled into vague background thoughts as their flight was announced and soon they had left the country.

Predictably, she talked about work on the trip over. She had shown a great deal of commendable initiative with one of his deals, presenting him with a list of facts and figures on a company he was in the middle of acquiring.

But she was awed by the whole first-class travelling experience. Gabriel was picking that up with antennae finely tuned to women and their responses. She wanted to play it cool, to keep that work hat firmly pinned in place, but she also wanted to stare around her at the plush surroundings, the muted subservience of the airline staff, the luxury...

They would be staying at one of the most expensive and high-profile hotels in Paris, a hotel that took luxury seriously. It was the only hotel in which he stayed when he was in the city and they knew how to look after him.

He felt a kick of pleasurable anticipation at seeing her face when they walked in.

He was a teenager again, trying hard to impress a girl...

Except, his teenage years had been a little too busy for such distractions. Escape had taken priority over making out with girls, not that that had been a problem for him. Besides, he wasn't in the business of impressing anybody. He didn't have to.

The limo that would be driving them wherever they wanted to go while they were in Paris was waiting for them at the airport when they arrived and Alice glanced over to him with a dry smile.

'Don't you *ever* do things the way most normal people do?' The question was directed more at herself than it had been to him, although he picked up the half-murmured remark and chose to answer as soon as they were in the back seat of the car.

'Why would I do that?' he asked with a careless shrug, angling his big body so that he was facing her. She had tucked her hair behind her ears and was wearing ear rings, little pearl studs that were a far cry from the wildly extravagant costume jewellery most girls her age would probably have worn.

Infused with silly holiday excitement, and guiltily feeling a bit like a princess after her first-class experience, now in this chauffeur-driven limo, Alice laughed.

'You don't do that enough,' Gabriel said gruffly, surprising himself with that observation, but meaning every syllable of it.

'Do what?' Alice rested back against the seat and looked at him through half-closed eyes.

'Laugh.'

'I didn't realise that being at work was a laugh-a-second experience,' she said, but there was no sarcasm in her voice which was lazy and relaxed. 'Do you do anything for yourself at all, Gabriel?' she mused aloud and he gave her a toe curlingly slow smile.

'I make money. A lot of it. Beyond that, I pay people to take care of everything else.'

'But surely that can't be satisfying all of the time?'

'Are you going to give me a mini-lecture on all the great things money can't buy?' He thought back to his fractured, troubled past. Money would have bought a hell of a lot for him back then, which was probably why he had become so intensely focused on making lots of it. 'Because, if you are, there's no way you can sell it to me.'

'Money can't buy love.'

This time Gabriel laughed out loud but there was an edge to his laughter that Alice picked up and her brown eyes were curious as they rested on his handsome face.

'Oh, but I've found just the opposite.'

'That's not love…' How had they ended up having this very personal conversation? She sat up and leaned against the car door.

'No, but it works for me,' Gabriel told her drily. He hadn't taken her for a romantic, but was she one at heart? Perhaps all women were. Or at least, they were in love with the idea of being in love: the excited trip to the jewellers; the wedding planning; the meringue of a white dress on the big day; the happy-ever-after, as if such a thing existed. The fact was, the relationships didn't last. They all collapsed in varying degrees. He was a prime example of that, although in his case the degree of collapse had been severe, if the two people who had stupidly had sex and produced him had ever had a relationship at all. It was doubtful, although that was something he would never know. He had been dumped as a baby, taken into care and his life had been kick-started from that point.

'What about marriage? Settling down?' She couldn't resist giving in to her curiosity and he raised his eyebrows questioningly.

'What about it?'

'Aren't you tempted at all…?'

'Not that I've ever noticed. I long ago came to the conclusion, my dear little secretary, that the one thing I can rely on is money. I know how to make it and I'm fully aware of the uses I can put it to. There are no unpredictable variants when it comes to money. It might be hard and cold but it doesn't make demands, it doesn't nag and it doesn't want what's not on the cards. It also...as you have experienced...buys me exactly what I want, when I want it.'

Alice had no illusions about love either, but neither was she steeped in cynicism, and she shivered involuntarily at the ice-cold centre she glimpsed inside him.

Not only did he not believe in love, he would never bother trying to find it. As far as he was concerned, it didn't exist. He made money, he paid people to take care of life's little inconveniences and he slept with women for physical release.

He was not one of life's good guys and how fair was it that, despite that, his raw sexuality made him a magnet that few could resist?

She turned away and stared out of the car window. It was a beautiful day with skies as clear and as blue here as they had been in London.

'Perhaps you could tell me what the plans are for today,' she suggested, pulling back from the conversation, although it lingered in her head like a song being played on a loop.

'Hotel. A few hours' respite. Then we will be taking the client out tonight.'

'I haven't booked anywhere.'

'Francois and Marie are entertaining us,' Gabriel informed her. 'At their home. Hence arriving today rather than Monday. The entire family will be there. I thought it might be an opportune moment to hear their various opinions on the company sale so that we can squash any last-minute nerves.'

'At their *house*?'

'Rumour has it that the place is palatial. I've been told by Francois that various important dignitaries will be there. They are celebrating their fortieth wedding anniversary; we're honoured to have been invited.'

Alice looked at him, alarmed. When it came to the client entertainment side of their stay in Paris, she had been thinking more along the lines of one or two stuffy restaurants where she could easily fade into the background—the ever-professional secretary tagging along to make notes.

She hadn't banked on anything too elaborate. Frantically trying to think what she could wear to somewhere palatial with circulating dignitaries, all thoughts left her head as the limo pulled up outside their hotel.

Lacking in money and poorly travelled as she was, Alice had still heard of this hotel. She paused and stared at the impressive building facing her and was even more impressed when she followed Gabriel inside.

Marble, chandeliers and stunning paintings and tapestries announced its enviable status as the very best anyone could get for their money.

'We're staying here?' she breathed, and Gabriel turned to her with a slight smile.

'If you can afford the very best, why not have it? You know by now that that's my mantra.'

Alice glanced at him. He was the very epitome of a man at ease in his surroundings. He accepted the sudden flurry of activity around him as his due. No one could bow too low or scrape too hard and she felt a thrilling little flutter at being the woman at his side.

Even if she was only here in her role as his valuable secretary.

'There's something I need to ask you,' she whispered as they were shown up to their adjoining suites.

'No need to whisper,' Gabriel whispered back. 'I very much doubt the bellboy is interested in anything we have to say. A poker face is essential in places like this. The truly wealthy seldom like to be gawped at.'

Alice's eyes flashed and he laughed. 'Should I apologise for my arrogance?' He briefly turned away and spoke fluently to the bellboy in French, who faded away with a slight bow and an ingratiating smile at the huge tip placed in his hand.

'I guess you're only being honest,' she reluctantly conceded. From what she could glimpse behind him, the room was spectacular. Huge, big enough for a separate little sitting room, and everything was decorated with decadent opulence.

'One of life's few true virtues: honesty. You said you had something to talk to me about…' He walked into the room, paying no attention at all to his surroundings, leading her to assume that he had been there many times before. 'Come in and spit it out.'

Alice hovered by the door as he pulled his jumper over his head and flung it on the bed which, like the room, was super-sized. In the process, his shirt was tugged out of the waistband of his trousers and she glimpsed a tantalising sliver of bronzed stomach, as flat and as hard as a washboard.

'Well?' Gabriel prompted. 'Don't just stand there.' He turned away and began scrolling down his Blackberry, frowning at emails as Alice tentatively walked into the room.

The presence of the bed was disconcerting. It brought back memories of the last time she had been in a bedroom with him, which was not what she wanted to think about.

When she was stranded in the middle of the room, he eventually glanced up and indicated one of the chairs which formed a little cluster by the window.

'I'm afraid I hadn't banked on us doing anything as fancy as dining out with…dignitaries,' she said without beating around the bush. 'I was under the impression that this was going to be all about work.'

'So you packed your grey suit, a couple of white blouses, some black tights and your black patent shoes…'

'I know it's boring, Gabriel, but I don't see work as a fashion parade!' Her face stung from the implied insult. 'If you had told me that—'

'You knew we would be entertaining this client,' Gabriel pointed out flatly. 'Surely you wouldn't have assumed that your work suits would do the trick?'

'Why not? They're smart and professional—'

'They're bland and drab.'

'I don't think that's fair at all!'

'You get exactly the same clothes allowance as the rest of my employees on your level, yet you don't appear to have spent a penny on clothes.'

Because she spent the money paying a professional to help her mother with her problem. Because, however much she was paid, by the time that money left her hands, given all the other bills, plus the little nest egg she was slowly accumulating, there was precious little left and none at all for jackets that cost five hundred pounds and designer shoes that could run to more.

'How do you know I haven't?'

'Well, unless you're throwing money at an exotic out of work wardrobe, it shows.'

'I didn't realise that there was a certain dress code to work for you.' But it was apparent all around her. She had noticed it on day one. 'And I don't think I should be channelled into wearing stuff I don't like because you say so.'

'Before this conversation starts drifting into territory I know I won't like,' Gabriel informed her coolly, 'I suggest you use what remains of the day to go shopping.'

Alice thought about the paucity of her funds and blanched. 'I…I would have to dip into my savings…'

Gabriel waved aside her faltering objection with an impatient wave of his hand.

'I will transfer money into your account today. Use it. Buy enough designer clothes to last the duration and feel free to make use of the spa centre here. Do whatever it takes.'

'Do whatever it takes…for what?' Alice said stiffly. If the ground had opened up, she would have dived in head first and emerged somewhere very far away from where this man was sitting, telling her in not so many words that she was an embarrassment.

'Alice,' Gabriel told her bluntly, 'you're a young girl in your twenties and I have yet to see you in something frivolous.'

'I would never come to work in anything frivolous.'

'Do you possess anything that isn't sober? Serious? *Grey*?' He knew he was being harsh but he had seen a hint of someone fiery lurking underneath the proper exterior and he wanted to see that person on the outside.

'Francois and Marie are rich and they're French. Put the two together and what you have is elegance. They will be startled if you appear at my side wearing off-the-peg cheap, ill-fitting grey suits. What you wear might not be a deal breaker, but it will help if you blend in. Do you really think that you can show up to tonight's event in a *suit*?'

Cheap, off-the-peg, ill-fitting… The words reverberated in her head until she was giddy with anger.

'I did think to bring my black dress.'

'I'm imagining it's along the same lines as the suit…?'

'By which,' Alice said tightly, 'you mean cheap, off-the-peg and ill-fitting?'

Gabriel raked long fingers through his dark hair and sighed heavily. 'I could have skirted round this,' he told her bluntly. 'I could have wrapped up what needed to be said in lots of pretty packaging, but that's not my style. If you wear one of those suits of yours, you will feel desperately uncomfortable the minute you step through their front door. I'm sparing you that ordeal by being honest. They will wonder what sort of employer I am if I don't pay my staff enough for them to afford decent clothing...'

'Do you have any idea just how *insulting* you're being right now?' She was close to tears but there was no way that she would allow them to spill over.

'Do you have any idea just how awkward you will feel if you arrive there and find that you're not blending in? That you're sticking out like a sore thumb?' His dark eyes challenged her to continue an argument which he knew he would win.

'And what exactly do you suggest I waste your money buying?'

'You're treading on thin ice here, Alice. I could suggest that you buy something dressy...colourful. Or else I could just tell you to—'

'I apologise if you think I'm being ungrateful or rude, Gabriel, but I resent being told what I can and can't wear!' But when she thought about entering a room full of elegant French people who were dressed to kill, in one of her suits or her very simple black dress, she knew that he had a point.

She just hated the way he felt free to tell her with no regard for her feelings at all. She resented the way he felt that he didn't even have to make a pretence of trying to be diplomatic.

'It is what it is.' But for once he was annoyed with himself for doing what he always did, for speaking his mind without window dressing what he had to say.

'Fine!'

She glowered at him and Gabriel was sorely tempted

to tell her that there wasn't a woman on the face of the earth who wouldn't have jumped at the chance to go out and have a shopping spree at his expense. Yet she had that 'just swallowed a lemon' look on her face as though he had somehow humiliated her in public. Hell, he was trying to *spare* her from being humiliated in public! People were shallow and one of the first things he had learnt in his climb up that swaying ladder was that they judged according to what they saw; forget all that claptrap about what was underneath. Dress and act like a king, and they would treat you like one.

Yet he was further annoyed when he felt another wave of guilt wash over him. She had been insulted, even though what he had said had been perfectly true.

He wasn't about to apologise even if she stood there glowering until kingdom come. He pointedly looked at his watch and told her that she should get her skates on if she intended to get through some shopping, then he recommended a couple of districts where designer shops lined the streets. He even told her she could take the limo

'And what time shall I meet you?' Alice could barely get the words out. She hadn't sat down, but had remained standing, and her legs were unsteady with sheer anger.

'The do kicks off at eight. Meet me in the bar here at seven-thirty. We can have a drink first and then get there around eight-thirty.'

Because, she sniped to herself, the great man could arrive late if he wanted. Forget about currying favour with the person whose company you wanted to buy! Currying favour was something only lesser mortals did! Gabriel Cabrera didn't feel he had to do that, so he didn't.

'And will we be doing any work before we leave?' she asked with wooden politeness.

'It's Saturday. I think I can spare you.'

'Fine.' She galvanised her legs into action and walked towards the door. She would have a shower, unpack some of her drab grey clothes to wear out and then she would hit the shops and spend that money he had made no bones about telling her she should spend—so that she could get herself up to scratch and blend in! 'I'll see you in the bar at seven-thirty. Perhaps you could let me know if there's a change of plan.'

She let herself out of the room without a backward glance. She had over-reacted, she knew that, but she had just lost her cool at the sheer arrogance and superiority of the man.

She showered quickly, barely paying any attention to the stunning bedroom she had been allocated, which was a mirror reflection of his, then out she went.

He wanted his drab secretary to do something about her appearance so that he didn't flinch when he looked at her?

Well, she would make sure she did her very best to do as he had asked!

CHAPTER FIVE

ALICE HAD NEVER, ever had anything that could possibly be called an unlimited budget when it came to buying clothes. Or buying anything, for that matter.

Growing up, her father's job had been good enough. He'd been a middle-management man who had paid the bills, given his wife just enough to get by and spent the remainder on pleasing himself. Holidays had just not happened. Or maybe they had, in the early days before she had come along, and perhaps when she had been a baby, too young to remember them. Maybe they had happened when her parents had been a happily married statistic instead of two opponents fighting their private cold war.

Pocket money for clothes had been thin on the ground. Her mother had passed her some, whatever was left from the housekeeping money at the end of the month, but Alice had never known what it was like to spend cash on things that weren't strictly necessary.

So it took her a little while to get her head round the fact that that was exactly what she had now been ordered to do.

She had brought a little pocket guide-book with her and, instead of rushing instantly to the shops, she took the limo to the Champs-Elysées, which was hardly necessary, considering how close their hotel was to it.

She wandered. She mingled in the glorious weather with the rich fashionistas. She walked past the expensive restaurants and cafés. There was no time to visit any of the museums but she could admire the architecture of some of the grand buildings and submerge herself in the airy affluence. She stopped to have a coffee and a croissant in one of the cafés and sat outside so that she could people watch.

In her head, she replayed every word Gabriel had said to her and relived the hurt she had felt at being dismissed as someone inferior. It didn't matter whether he praised her work skills to the skies. It didn't matter if he complimented her on her initiative in digging out bits of useful information on companies he was interested in acquiring. It didn't matter if he now trusted her to flesh out reports which he gave to her in skeleton format.

She was the drab, grey little person who didn't know how to dress.

She had a flashback of Georgia in the office, in her tight red dress and her high, high shoes, with her dark hair everywhere and her long nails painted scarlet.

There was no way that Alice would want to replicate that look. As far as she was concerned, the other woman had embodied everything that was obvious and way too out there.

But she wasn't going to be a mouse.

It took her a little while, but by the time she hit the fourth shop she was in her stride. She cruised through all the designer shops, growing in confidence as the afternoon wore on, and by five o'clock she returned to the hotel clutching several bags. She could have summoned the limo again but the walk had been tempting, if tiring.

And what better place to soothe a weary body? She dumped the bags in her bedroom, inhaled the gorgeous opulence of a hotel room the likes of which she would never stay in again for a few heady minutes and then phoned through to make an appointment at the hotel pa.

By six-thirty, Alice was fully rested and relaxed. Back in her room, she looked at her nails, her feet, her hair.

Vanity had never been a problem for her. As a teenager, when all the other girls had been preening in front of mirrors and whispering about boys she had been busy keeping her head down, studying and wondering what the following day would bring; wondering what sort of mood her mother might be in or whether her father might be on one of his many 'time out' trips.

The years had passed her by without her taking time out to pay much attention to her appearance.

Besides, her learning curve had been subtle but powerful. Beauty came with a price. She wasn't beautiful and she had no interest in making herself try to be.

But now…

She had a long, lingering bath in a bathroom that was ridiculously luxuriant and emerged twenty minutes later feeling refreshed and…weirdly excited.

She wasn't Cinderella going to the ball—not exactly—but she would leave behind serious, composed, take-no-risks Alice Morgan for the evening.

She had bought four dresses, one for each evening they would be in Paris, but the dress she had bought for tonight's affair was the dressiest.

It was a long dress, in the palest of pink, with a scooped neck and was figure-hugging. Her long body, which she had always considered far too thin and far too flat-chested, filled it out perfectly and her height was accentuated by four-inch stilettos. She had bought a matching cashmere throw, iridescent with little pearls, to sling over her shoulders. Her nails matched the outfit and her hair…

Her brown hair, always *au naturel*, had been highlighted

while she had had her hands and feet done. Shades of warm chestnut and caramel streaked through it, giving it dazzling life, turning her into a person she barely recognised as herself.

On the spur of the moment, she took a picture of herself and messaged it to her mother, and grinned when her mother returned a message which was just several exclamation marks.

She was a different person, at least on the surface, and she left her bedroom at precisely seven-thirty to make her way downstairs to the bar.

People turned to stare.

That had never happened to her in her life before. She wasn't sure whether she liked it or not but it was certainly an experience.

Was this what it was like for Gabriel? she wondered. Was that why he had become so lazy? Why he picked what he wanted from life and discarded the rest without a backward glance? Was he so accustomed to walking into a room and finding himself the focus of attention that he no longer saw the point of trying any more? Why seek people out when they sought *you* out? Why make an effort with a woman if the woman was happy to do all the chasing? Why commit to a relationship when you could treat life like a great big candy shop where you could pick and choose the candy you wanted before moving on to sample something else?

She wondered whether he got pleasure from making money. He had made so much already and at such a young age, more than enough to last several lifetimes. He threw himself into his work, there was no denying that, and the man was a genius with a knack of knowing the markets— but did it still give him a kick? When you could have whatever you wanted without trying, was there *anything* that was still capable of giving you a kick?

She had to ask directions to the bar and, when she got there, she paused and frankly gaped.

It was carpeted, the carpet pale, patterned and very old. On the walls, deep, rich tapestries left you in no doubt that this hotel was old and proud of its age. Rich velvet curtains hung at the long windows and the chairs were regal, blending in with the air of expensive antiquity. There were no modern touches, nothing to indicate that outside the bustling twenty-first century was happening.

It was fabulous French decadence. It recalled the days of aristocracy and noblemen.

At which point, she scanned the room and there he was, sitting at one of the tables, frowning in front of the newspaper.

Temporarily lost in the financial section of the newspaper he was reading, absently drinking a glass of red wine from the bottle that had been placed on the table in front of him, Gabriel was unaware of her entrance.

And of the heads turning in her direction as she stood by the door looking at him.

But gradually he picked up that there was a certain silence. His eyes unerringly found her and for a few seconds he found that he was holding his breath.

He half-stood, which she took as a signal to move forward to join him, and although his breath returned he couldn't tear his eyes away from her slowly approaching figure. He was aware of men turning to stare.

'So...' he drawled when she was standing in front of him. 'You obeyed my instructions to the letter.' She was exquisite. How had he failed to notice that before? The pale delicacy of her features was a revelation, as was the slender column of her neck, the graceful elegance of her body. Her presence dominated the room even though what she had chosen to wear was simple, unrevealing and refined.

'You told me to get rid of my drab, grey clothes...'
Was that all he could say? she thought with a stab of disappointment.

'Glass of wine?' He sat back down, inwardly marvelling that she had managed to puncture his composure. 'Where did you go shopping?'

Alice sat and gave him a little run-down of how she had spent her afternoon. Had he been staring at her as she had walked towards him? Or had he only been just looking to make sure that she could pass muster? His expression had been unreadable and she had a fierce longing for him to tell her that she looked beautiful.

He, of course, looked as stunning as he always did. He was dressed semi-formally in a charcoal-grey suit that looked hand-tailored and lovingly accentuated his physique.

'Your hair...' he murmured. 'Very effective.'

Alice blushed, no longer feeling like his secretary but feeling, weirdly, like his date, even though she recognised the foolishness of letting herself get swept away by such a silly notion.

'I had it dyed,' she confessed self-consciously. 'I hope it's not too much.'

'It's...' Gabriel was momentarily lost for words. 'It's... It suits you.' He fought the temptation to reach out and run his fingers through its silky length.

'Should we perhaps run through what sort of questions we might get asked about this buy-out?'

Gabriel found that he couldn't care less about the buy-out. For once, business could not have been further from his mind. Those little snippets of wayward thoughts that had flitted through his mind now and again—little snapshots of her released from her armour of the perfect little secretary—coalesced into one powerful image of her without that dress on, naked and sprawled on his bed…

And where was he going with that thought, exactly? He had always made it his business never to mix work with pleasure—that was a sure-fire recipe for problems. The sexy little thing in the accounts department might display her wares but those were offers he had always avoided like the plague.

But this woman…

'Yes,' he murmured. 'We should do that—discuss potential problems; try and cut them off at the pass…' He drained his glass and poured himself another. Potential problems? Who cared? He had it covered. His mind wanted to think about other intriguing possibilities…

He half-listened as she launched into a summary of the company and the technicalities of buying something that was rooted in a family.

'Especially when there are…how many children did you say…? Three? All involved in the decision-making process…?'

'Three children, yes,' Gabriel murmured, sitting back and sipping his wine. It took extreme will power not to let his eyes rove over her pert breasts. She was so unlike the women he'd dated who had all been universally proud of the fact that they spilled out of bras. Since when, he mused, was that such a great selling point anyway? 'Two boys and a girl,' he added, because she seemed to expect him to expand on that succinct statement. 'And I gather the daughter doesn't really care one way or another. She travels, it would seem, spreading peace and love and playing at being a trust-fund hippy. What about you? Any siblings?'

'I beg your pardon?'

'We're sitting here, having a drink. We don't have to spend our time discussing work.' He topped up her glass, gently pushing aside her hand which she had raised to stop him. 'Tell me about your family. Brothers? Sisters? Usual assortment of nieces and nephews, cousins and aunts and uncles wheeled out on high days and holidays?'

Alice felt the little pulse at the side of her neck beating steadily. Her mother was an only child and her father had a brother in Australia whom, he had always been very proud to say, he loathed. When she had been younger, she had longed for a brother or a sister. As time had gone by, she had ditched those dreams. What if a brother had turned out like her father? No, theirs had always been an unhappy little family unit, marooned on open water without the benefit of a neighbouring craft to help pick up the pieces should anything happen. As it had.

He was simply being polite, and she was hardly confessing to state secrets, but it still felt awkward to start talking to him about her private life. She needed those boundaries between them to be kept in place or else it would be so much more difficult to keep the attraction she felt towards him at bay.

Hadn't she already fluttered like a girl on her first date? Hadn't she wanted him to *notice* her, and not just as his efficient secretary? She was in dangerous territory and control came from not forgetting their respective roles.

But if she dodged his question she'd stir his curiosity and he was tenacious, a dog with a bone, when it came to finding out things he wanted to find out.

'I'm—I'm an only child,' she told him haltingly. 'My father's dead. A car accident.'

'I'm sorry.' Though the way she had said that… 'And your mother?'

'Lives in Devon.' She took two small sips of wine and offered him a bright, brittle smile.

'Has the polite conversation come to an end?' he asked.

'I've just had a look at the clock behind you and it's time for us to go.' She stood up and carefully avoided looking at him as she smoothed down her dress. When she raised her eyes, it was to find his on her and he didn't look away. He just kept looking until colour crawled into her cheeks, her mouth went dry and her brains turned to cotton wool.

Confusion paralysed her. Was he looking at her *that* way? The way she tried hard not to look at him?

'You look quite…stunning,' he murmured, extending his arm and then tucking her arm into the crook of his.

'Thank you,' Alice croaked. She wasn't sure what she was finding more disastrous on her nerves, the fact that she had her arm looped through his or the fact that he had just delivered the compliment she had been desperate to hear with a look in his eyes that had made her whole body tingle with forbidden awareness.

Maybe it was a look that he pulled out of the box whenever he saw any woman who didn't look half bad.

'Even though,' she continued, weakly asserting her independence, 'I still disapprove of you telling me what I can or can't wear.'

'Even though you're surely going to be the belle of the ball?'

'Oh, please!' She tried to dismiss that husky compliment with a laugh.

'You don't believe me?' They were at the limo, which had appeared as if by magic, and the chauffeur swooped round to open the door for her.

'I…no…maybe. I don't know.' Her voice was low, breathless and husky. Nothing at all like how she usually sounded. It was a voice that matched her beautiful Cinderella dress. Her eyes were wide, her pupils dilated as she stared at him, riveted by the beautiful, hard planes of his face and by the way he was still looking at her.

She heard something come from her, something soft and low, and recognised with horror that it was a moan, barely audible, but as loud as clanging bells in her own ears.

Gabriel knew this moment for what it was. Her pliant, warm body was inches away from his. They were leaning into one another, driven by some unseen current. If he turned away right now he would break the spell and that would be the best thing to do.

She was his secretary! And a damned good one. Did he want to jeopardise that by starting something he would not be able to finish? Something that would end in her being hurt, in walking out on him? Wasn't this the very reason there was such a thing as lines that should never get crossed?

He kissed her.

Long, slowly, lingeringly, his tongue probing into her mouth, tasting her sweetness and hardening as she moaned back into his mouth.

Hell, they were in the back seat of a car! He was not cool or controlled, but he couldn't help himself as he cupped one small, rounded breast and rubbed his finger over the nipple which he could feel pressing against the fabric.

'You're not wearing a bra...' He was turned on beyond belief. Her nipple was hard and he was gripped with an insane urge to tell the driver to turn around so that he could take her back to his hotel room and...have her. Rip the dress off her, get her down to her underwear and take her as fast and as hard as he could.

'The back of the dress is too low...' She didn't want him to talk. She wanted him to carry on kissing her. Her whole body was on fire, as though she had been plugged into a live socket. Her nerve-endings were charged, her thoughts sluggish, the blood hot in her veins.

She felt the heaviness of his hand resting on her thigh,

gently pressing, edging between her legs, and sanity shot through her. She pulled back and made a show of straightening her dress, giving herself time to come to her senses.

Her breasts were tingling and her nipples pinching from where he had touched her.

What the heck had she done?

'What's the matter?' Gabriel was so turned on that he could hardly string that simple sentence together. He wasn't sure whether it was the taste of the forbidden, or the fact that she was a novelty after a steady diet of Georgia clones, but he had never been so turned on in his life before.

'*What's the matter?* What do you *think* the matter is, Gabriel?' She glanced furtively at the chauffeur but he was seemingly indifferent to what had taken place in the back seat of the limo. Gabriel was right—underlings knew the wisdom of playing dead when it came to the shenanigans of their wealthy employers.

'I have no idea,' Gabriel drawled, settling back against the car door to look at her calmly. 'One minute you were kissing me and the next minute you'd decided to play the outraged virgin. What blew the fire out?'

How could he sit there and look at her as though she had made a mistake with her typing, misfiled something or put through the wrong call? How could he be so...*cool*?

'That should never have happened,' Alice told him tautly. 'And it wouldn't have happened if I hadn't had two glasses of wine.'

'One and a half, and if you kiss men after a glass and a half of wine what do you do after a bottle? There's nothing worse than a woman who blames alcohol for doing something she actually wanted to do but then had second thoughts about doing.'

Alice reddened. 'Well, it won't happen again. I made

a mistake and I won't be repeating it. And I don't want it mentioned ever again.'

'Or else…?'

'Or else my position with you will become untenable and I don't want that to happen. I like my job. I don't want one small, tiny error of judgement to end up spoiling that.'

Gabriel allowed the silence to lengthen between them until she was compelled to look at him, if only to find out whether he had heard what she had just said.

One small, tiny error of judgement, he thought, amused at her naivety in assuming that she could shut the door on what had happened and pretend it hadn't happened. She had wanted him. Her warm body had curved into his and he had felt her desire throbbing through her, hot, wet and feverish. If he had slipped his hand under that long dress, if he had found the bareness of her thighs, he would have found her ready for him.

'I don't suppose you've ever had any woman say that to you before.' Alice broke the silence which was driving her crazy. 'And I don't want to offend you, but that's how it has to be.'

'In response to that statement, you're right. I've never had a woman say that to me before. I'm not offended.' He raised both his hands in a gesture that was rueful but accepting. 'And of course, if you decide that denial is the right course of action, then that's not a problem. We'll pretend it never happened.'

'Good.' She felt a hollowness settle in the pit of her stomach.

'There's our destination straight ahead.' Gabriel pointed to the bank of lights leading up a tree-lined avenue towards a manor house that resembled the Place des Vosges. Expensive cars were dotted around the courtyard and along the avenue, half on, half off the grass verge. He began giving her a potted history of the place, which had been in the family for generations.

But he was alive to her presence next to him. She had opened a door and he had walked through; did she now expect him politely to turn around and walk back out because she'd had a change of heart?

Frankly, if he believed for a second that her response had been wine induced, he would not have hesitated to put their five-minute interaction down to experience.

But she had wanted him and she still did. He could feel it in the way she wasn't quite managing to look at him, in her breathing which she was trying to control, in the way she was ever so casually pressed against the car door. It was almost as though if she got too close to him she would burst into flame. All over again.

Any thoughts about walking away from this challenge vanished in a puff of smoke. The predator in him prowled to the fore, leaving no room for questions about the fool-hardiness of what he wanted to do.

For once, there was something in him that wasn't in control and he liked it. It made a change and a change was as good as a rest.

The party was in full swing when they walked in. Beautiful people were circulating, chatting in groups, drinking champagne and picking off the canapés that were being paraded from group to group by a selection of very attractive waitresses. They were all dressed in just the sort of sexy uniform associated with the French waitress: short skirt, tight black top, high black shoes and sheer black stockings.

Gabriel barely noticed them. Alice was the sole recipient of his brooding attention.

She did him proud, it had to be said. Men looked, as did the women. She shone. And, if her grasp of French was classroom, she charmingly made the most of what was at her disposal as she was adopted by groups of people and encouraged to join their conversations.

And the deal was cemented. The family, Francois told him, taking him to one side towards the end of the evening, was behind him all the way. There were some regrets about losing the business but he intended to join his sons in a new start-up, completely different, in the leisure industry.

Gabriel had expected nothing but a positive outcome and he was ready to make his exit when he scanned the room to see Alice laughing, deep in conversation with a man. A tall, blond man who was watching her over the rim of his flute as he drank his champagne in a way that Gabriel recognised all too well. She was laughing.

Rage tore through him.

He made his way through the thinning crowds. The noise level was high. People had had a lot to drink. Hell, *she* had had a lot to drink!

He descended on them like an avenging angel and cupped her elbow in the palm of his big hand.

'Time to go, Alice.'

'Already?' There was still that laughter in her eyes as she turned to look at him. Her face was flushed, her full mouth parted, inviting…

'Already,' Gabriel gritted. He spoke to the blond guy in rapid French and then waited in silence as the other man replied and then, when nothing further was forthcoming, made his apologies, taking her hand and kissing it in a way that smacked of unwelcome intimacy.

'We're going to bid our farewells to our charming hosts.' He still had his hand on her elbow and was channelling her towards Francois and Marie who were standing in the centre of the room, surrounded by their friends and family. 'And then we're going to head back to our hotel.'

'Hasn't it been a fantastic affair?'

'Who the hell was that loser you were talking to?' He plastered a polite smile on his face as they approached their hosts, and kept smiling as he thanked them for a wonderful time, to be repaid in full when they were next in London. Arrangements were made for meetings on Monday. He didn't take his hand away from her.

'That,' he said, dropping her elbow as they walked out into the cool late night air, 'was not what I brought you here to do.' In his mind's eye, he saw her laughing face as she looked up at Prince Charming of the floppy blond hair.

Alice laughed. The champagne had gone to her head, as had the fact that she had only had a handful of the delicious canapés being passed around. The memory of that searing kiss in the back seat of the limo, her confusion at what had promoted it and sheer nerves at being somewhere so utterly out of her comfort zone had combined and she had drank far more than she usually did.

'You wanted me to dress the part and mingle...'

'I wanted you to stay by my side and listen so that you could make mental notes of what was said about the deal!' He waited until she was in the passenger seat, indicating to the chauffeur to remain where he was, and slammed the door behind her.

'I did *not* expect you to drink like a fish and start cosying up to random men!'

Alice swivelled to look at his hard, unyielding profile. 'I wasn't *drinking like a fish* or *cosying up to random men*,' she protested. She sensed the tension in his bunched shoulders and sat on her treacherous hands, because more than anything else she wanted to touch him and that wasn't going to do.

'Who was that guy? Did he have anything to contribute on my acquisition of Francois' company?'

'Well, no...' She stifled a yawn and was treated to a thunderous glare.

'Am I keeping you awake? Maybe you've forgotten that you're being paid a hefty amount of money for the inconvenience of losing your weekend.' He knew he sounded like a tyrant but he wasn't about to back down. She looked sleepy-eyed and just so damned sexy...

'I would have stuck to you like glue if you had made it clear that that was what you wanted, but I gathered...' she stifled another yawn, which didn't go unnoticed '...that this was a social event. Besides, I didn't notice you in any tête-à-têtes with Monsieur Armand or I would have come over. I know I'm being paid a lot for my overtime here. You don't have to remind me.'

Gabriel couldn't care less about the money and she wasn't saying anything he wanted to hear. Who was that guy? Had she answered *that* question? No. Had telephone numbers been exchanged? Had some kind of date been set up?

'So who was he?' he asked through gritted teeth.

'Are you...*jealous*?' Her lips parted and she was suddenly as sober as a judge.

'Did you exchange numbers? Set up a hot date for later in the week? If so, you can forget it. You're going nowhere on company time.' He raked his fingers though his hair and stared at her with frowning intensity.

He had never been jealous in his life before. He didn't do jealousy. Why would he? Women came and they went and, whatever the pasts were, whoever they had been out with or spoke to, well, he had never cared. Nor had he ever doubted that once they were in his bed they were utterly faithful.

He was jealous now and he didn't like the sensation.

'Of course I didn't give Marc my telephone number,'

Alice muttered, half-resenting that she had been called to task like a kid, half-thrilled because, whatever he said or didn't say, he *was* jealous. It made her feel better about fancying him. At least she knew that he wasn't as casual about it as he had pretended.

Not that it mattered, one way or another.

'And there are no hot dates lined up. He was just a nice man who didn't mind talking to me in pigeon French.'

Gabriel thought that there was a lot more the guy wouldn't have minded doing, given half a chance, but no numbers had been exchanged, no hot dates lined up. She seemed blissfully unaware that looking the way she did and laughing the way she had would be considered flirting in any language, pigeon or not.

'You asked me if I was jealous,' Gabriel murmured, keeping his distance but looking at her with dark intensity. 'I was jealous.'

The atmosphere between them shifted and changed into something so charged that it was almost tangible. Alice drew her breath in sharply and then exhaled it in a shudder. Wild horses wouldn't drag this out of her, but she had been keeping an eye on him throughout the evening, waiting to see if he looked at any of the glamorous women there or any of the pretty young waitresses. He had garnered enough attention, although if he had noticed any of it he hadn't shown it.

'Why?' She strove to remember the boundary lines between them and to summon up the will power she had shown earlier when she had told him that that one kiss had been a mistake, never to be repeated.

'Because I want you.' His body language was a heady turn-on; he was leaning indolently against the car door while he continued to watch her with still, lazy eyes.

'We can't do anything,' she said huskily. 'It would be a terrible mistake. I'm just not that type of girl.'

'The type who sleeps with a man if she wants to? And don't try telling me that you don't want to.'

'We shouldn't be having this conversation.'

'And your vocabulary shouldn't be littered with so many shoulds and shouldn'ts...'

'You're accustomed to women dropping at your feet.'

'And yet I haven't noticed you dropping at mine.'

The limo pulled up outside the hotel. He hadn't even noticed the journey. Every nerve and fibre in his body had honed in on the woman sitting as far as she could away from him.

He leaned forward to have a word with the driver and then they were walking up to the hotel entrance, several feet between them. He had his hands in his pockets and she was clutching her pink pearl throw and little handbag for dear life.

He was jealous...a first.

He was in pursuit...also a first.

And he would have her...but she would come to him.

CHAPTER SIX

ALICE COULD HEAR the beating of her own heart as they headed for their respective bedrooms. It was still relatively busy in the foyer, but once they left that behind the silence between them was deafening.

In fact, she wondered whether she had imagined the bizarre conversation they had just had. She couldn't bring herself to look at him, but it didn't matter, because in the quiet of the lift his image was reflected back at her whether she liked it or not.

She, standing by the door, arms wrapped round her body… He, leaning against the mirrored wall, hands in his pockets, dark, lean face sending shivers up and down her spine.

The doors pinged open and she leapt out. Her feet were aching from wearing high shoes and on the spur of the moment she stooped and took them off so that the long dress pooled on the ground.

'Undressing already?' Gabriel murmured in a sinfully seductive voice.

'My feet are killing me. I'm not used to wearing heels.'

'Well, give them a good night's rest and I shall see you in the morning.' He inclined his head politely, spun round on his heels and started walking towards his bedroom which was a little further up from hers.

And tomorrow, Alice thought feverishly, all this would be forgotten. That kiss in the back of the limo…the way he had looked at her…their conversation after the party: it would all be forgotten in the cold, clear light of day because that was just how things were.

She was the perfect secretary and if, by some weird twist of fate, he made her feel young and alive and filled with possibilities then that was something she would have to set to one side.

Maybe even to learn from it.

If a man whose value system left her cold managed to rouse her the way he did, then it was time for her to do something about getting her toes wet in the dating game instead of gathering cobwebs on the hard shoulder.

Shoes in hand, she watched as he fished into his jacket pocket for the key to his door. He wasn't even looking at her. He was going to shut that door behind him and…

She would never know.

'Wait!'

Gabriel turned slowly and smiled. Had he known that she would stop him? For once, he had been faced with an unpredictable outcome and he really wasn't sure what he would have done if she had struck off to her own room, shoes in hand, to get a good night's sleep and rest her feet.

He wasn't sure whether a few cold showers would dampen his raging libido.

'Yes?'

Alice sprinted towards him. It was funny but she hadn't realised how old she was in her behaviour, in her whole outlook on life, until he had come along and shaken her up so that everything had gone topsy-turvy and then re-settled, but in different positions.

She was twenty-five years old—when was the last time she had had an adventure?

She stood in front of him and looked up. 'Okay.'

'Okay...?'

'You know what I'm talking about. I...I'm attracted to you and I really don't understand why. You're not my type at all.'

'Promising start. That way, you won't start getting ideas.'

'What sort of ideas? Oh, forget I asked. Georgia-type ideas about having you around for longer than five seconds and getting attached and projecting into a non-existent future.' She laughed edgily. 'I work for you, remember? I'm not that stupid.'

'What's brought about the change of mind? I thought after we kissed that I was under instructions to forget about it immediately and pretend it had never happened.' He pushed open the bedroom door and stepped inside, switching on the light at the same time, then immediately dimming it to a mellow glow.

The bed had been turned back, not that there had been any need, and her pulses picked up their tempo as she looked at it—king-sized and beckoning her like a dangerous dare.

'Well?' he prompted, walking towards the sofa and flopping down on it, legs apart, arms resting loosely along the back.

'I...I suppose this is a one-off for me, and I know it's not a good idea, but...'

'Life is always full of *buts*,' Gabriel agreed. 'That's what makes it so challenging.' Except, truthfully, it contained relatively few buts for him, especially where a woman was involved. He had never had to try, so he hadn't. His emotional life had never contained any areas of hesitations and certainly no *buts*.

Silence settled between them and then he said softly, 'Take off your clothes.'

'What?'

'Let me see you naked, in front of me.'

'I…I can't.'

'Why not?' Something suddenly struck him: her inno-cence. The way she blushed, the hint of unbearable youth lurking underneath the professional exterior. 'You're not a virgin, are you?'

'Would it make a difference if I was?'

'Yes.' He sat forward, alert. 'It would.'

'Why?' She edged towards him and dropped the shoes on the floor. It would have felt strange to have plonked her-self next to him on the sofa so she sat on one of the chairs.

Talking was giving her time to doubt her decision. If she had fallen passionately into bed with him, she wouldn't have had time to think, but maybe this was a good thing. Maybe they both *needed* to talk, because this was not an ordinary situation, and a lot could change for the worse in its aftermath.

'Are you getting cold feet?' He shot her a crooked smile, reading her mind as though her thoughts had been writ-ten on her forehead, and that smile sealed her decision.

'No. Tell me why it would matter if I was a virgin.'

'You know me.' And she did, strangely. They worked so closely together and, although their working relationship was still new, he had the feeling that she *got* him. 'I'm not looking for…anything. It's what I tell every single woman I have ever dated and it's what I'm telling you now. Sex is a pleasurable pastime, but it's not love and it's not commit-ment, and it's not…going anywhere… If you're not experi-enced enough to take that on board…' He shrugged but his dark eyes were glued to her face. 'My…past experiences have not programmed me for any kind of commitment.'

'I'm not a virgin,' Alice told him abruptly. 'And talking about this makes it feel like an arrangement.'

'And that's a bad thing because…?'

'Because…' She faltered, thinking of the right way to say what she wanted to say, and he stepped into the breach without hesitation.

'Because you're looking for romance?'

'No! This is crazy. I'm going to go now. I should never have—'

Gabriel reached forward and circled her wrist with his hand and Alice shivered. Talking was a mood killer, whether it made sense or not. But that touch, the heat of his skin against hers, reminded her why she had stopped him in his tracks before he could enter his bedroom.

'Come closer and I'll show you why this might be crazy but why you shouldn't walk away.'

Mesmerised, Alice leaned towards him and half-closed her eyes. His cool lips against hers sent an explosion through her. She slid trembling fingers through his hair and caressed his neck. She could hardly believe what she was doing.

Was this really *her?* She wasn't a risk taker. Her life had been too unsteady for her to nurture the sort of devil-may-care attitude that encouraged spontaneous, careless behaviour. She was cautious, careful…

Yet she knew that she was about to take the biggest risk of her life in doing this and she didn't want to stop.

She kissed him slowly, drowning in the sensuality of his tongue melding with hers. As she kissed him, eyes closed, she blindly traced the contours of his beautiful face with her fingers. The wrap had slid off her shoulders and his hands were moving along her collarbone.

He drew back and she looked at him, still dazed from sensations she had never felt before.

'Undress for me, Alice…and don't tell me that you can't. Turn around. I'll unzip you.'

'I've never done a striptease before.'

'I'll show you how, in that case.' He stood up and began undressing. Very slowly, watching her as she watched him, her mouth half-open, fascination oozing from every pore.

Did it get better than this? Gabriel couldn't remember the last time he had been this turned on. She had the starstruck expression of a kid in a candy shop and it went to his head faster than a dose of adrenaline.

When his shirt was off, he began unzipping his trousers, and he grinned when she half-looked away, then looked back, then looked away again and finally returned her riveted gaze to his semi-clad body.

He was down to his boxers—dark-striped, silk boxers. Alice thought she might pass out. He had the highly toned body of an athlete: broad shoulders and a muscular torso that tapered down to a washboard-flat stomach and lean hips. Even in the most unforgiving of lights, he would still be beautiful.

Nerves gripped her.

What would he think of *her*? Was she opening herself up to humiliation? He might have waxed lyrical about finding her attractive, but it wouldn't do to forget that he went for small, voluptuous women with big breasts.

He didn't take off the boxers. Instead, he sat back down on the sofa and said with a wicked grin, 'Have I set an acceptable benchmark?'

Alice unzipped her dress herself. It was a long zip and it slid smoothly apart. She took a deep breath and then unlooped first one shoulder, then the other.

Another deep breath then it was off, sliding to the ground, the cool air hitting her bare breasts. He had looked at her with gleaming self-confidence when he had removed his clothes. She had her eyes shut until she heard him warmly, unsteadily tell her to open them.

The gentleness in his voice was like the waving of a magic wand and in that instant she shed her nerves as smoothly and as easily as she had shed her beautiful Cinderella dress.

She walked towards him wearing only her lacy pink panties and breathed in sharply as his hands settled on her hips and he sat up so that he could trail delicate kisses over her flat stomach.

She might not be a curvy Marilyn Monroe but she really turned him on. She could feel it in the way his hands shook ever so slightly and the way his breathing was just a little uncontrolled. Just for a brief window in time, her big, powerful boss was not the man who ruled the world but someone very human, someone driven by responses he couldn't tame, and she had done that. Her self-confidence soared.

'You're beautiful,' she heard him breathe.

She gripped his sinewy shoulders as he hooked his fingers into the waistband of her panties and tugged them down. She was completely naked and she didn't want to run for cover.

Two fumbling encounters with Alan before being ditched for a sexier model had left Alice with a punishing lack of self-confidence. If someone had told her that she would be able to do this—to stand in front of one of the sexiest men she could ever hope to meet and not feel embarrassed at her body—she would have laughed in disbelief. But that was exactly what she was doing now.

He parted her thighs with his hand and she curled her fingers into his hair and gasped as he traced the folds of her womanhood with his tongue. When he slipped it into her moistness, her legs almost gave way. The pleasure was unbearable.

This was refined torture as he teased her, bringing her

to dizzy heights before allowing her to subside. She was wet, throbbing, aching from wanting more.

He lifted her onto the bed and then laid her down and looked at her.

Her body was slim and graceful. Her breasts were just the right size. Her hair was like spun silk. He stepped out of his boxers. He was so hard for her that it was going to be a challenge to stop himself from doing the unthinkable; he knew that if she just touched him there he would release his seed like a teenager with no control.

Alice could scarcely breathe. She was overwhelmed with excitement. It coursed through her veins like a drug, washing away everything in its rampaging path. She had to squirm and resist touching herself to try to staunch the throbbing.

He settled on the bed and straddled her. She reached to touch him and he stayed her hand.

'No way.' Gabriel barely recognised the shakiness in his voice. 'If you do... I'm too turned on...'

'That's nice.'

'It's better than nice,' he growled in response. He lowered himself over her and she sighed and wriggled when he began teasing her breasts with his tongue.

'Hands above your head,' he commanded. Her nipples were big, pink discs and he tasted them delicately before taking one into his mouth and suckling on it, not letting up, enjoying her whimpers of delight and the way she moved, unable to keep still.

If she felt like a kid in a candy shop, then that was how he felt as well. The novelty of it was incredible, invigorating, exceptional.

When he could no longer bear the foreplay, he fumbled for his wallet, which he had dropped on the bedside table, and removed a condom.

Through the haze of her desire, Alice recognised a guy who took no chances. When he said that he did not involve himself in relationships for the long haul, he wasn't kidding.

She propped herself up on her elbows and watched as he put it on, fast and expertly. He was so big that she marvelled that he had not had any unfortunate accidents in the past from splitting one of them.

Their eyes met for the briefest of moments and he grinned.

'No risks, right?' she asked lightly and he nodded.

'Never.'

He nudged into her and then pushed harder so that she felt every bit of his girth rubbing inside her, sending waves of sensations shooting through her body. She clung. It was all she could do. Her short nails dug into his back as he moved harder and harder. Her legs wrapped round him and their bodies fused into one.

Her orgasm was deep, long and mind-blowing. Alice felt as if she was flying, soaring upwards, splintering into a thousand exquisite pieces. Her body arched as wave upon wave of unbearable pleasure coursed through her. One final thrust and he came as well, rearing up and groaning. Shudders of release ripped through his big body.

Unbelievable.

'Did the earth move for you?' he asked roughly, half-joking, half-serious, because it had damn well moved for *him*.

They had rolled onto their sides and were facing one another. It seemed perfectly natural. She had to lower her eyes because she felt so...*tender* towards him. That perfect moment of coming together was one of the few times when his guard was completely down, she suspected, and she supposed that it was the same for her. Now it was time for them to retreat to the people they were and tenderness didn't play any part in that.

'Shall I tell you how good you are?' she murmured teasingly and he clasped her fingers between his and kissed them one by one.

'That would be nice, and you can take your time. Feel free to be as descriptive as you like.'

'You're so egotistic, Gabriel.'

'Don't tell me you don't like it.' He kissed her and then settled his hand comfortably between her thighs. 'In fact, you have to tell me that you like it. I'm your boss.'

A timely reminder. She rolled onto her back and stared up at the ornate ceiling.

In the act of making love, she had lost the ability to think, but she was thinking now, remembering what he had said to her, how he had warned her off involvement: his little 'don't get attached to me' speech, the same little speech he would deliver to all his bed mates, of which she was now one.

Well, she might number among them, but she wasn't about to join their ranks in wanting more than he could give. She wasn't going to turn into another hysterical Georgia who had been silly enough to think that she could domesticate the jungle animal.

'You are,' she agreed lightly. 'Which is why this is only going to last for the duration of Paris.' Belatedly it occurred to her that she might have been a one-night stand. Had she jumped to the wrong conclusion?

'Is that a fact?' Gabriel murmured. He withdrew his hand to cup one breast instead and he gently stroked her until her nipple hardened.

'Being here is like playing truant…time off from normality.' Alice knew her body was reacting with wild abandon even though her voice was calm and controlled. She wanted him to flick his tongue over the tender nub of her nipple as he had done earlier; she wanted him to lick her between her legs until she couldn't breathe properly and then she wanted him inside her all over again, thrusting hard and sending her into glorious orbit.

Four days with him wasn't what she wanted but there was no way that she was going to lose control. She wasn't going to become his puppet.

And she wasn't going to let herself fall into the trap of thinking that, because maybe she had been harder to get than he was used to, he somehow was no longer the lazy guy who took what was on offer because he couldn't be bothered with the tedium of pursuit. She wasn't going to be another idiot who thought that he was capable of change.

'Normality being…?'

'Normality being London and the fact that I work for you. I'm being serious, Gabriel. I don't want to jeopardise my job. I can't think when you're doing…*that*…' He had slipped his fingers inside her and was absently teasing her tender, sensitive flesh.

'That suits me,' he drawled and Alice fought down the sudden flare of irrational disappointment. 'You're the best secretary I've ever had.'

'And besides,' she said drily, 'you like a quick turnaround when it comes to women, don't you?'

'Always.' Gabriel thought it best to remind her, although she was not like the other women he had been out with. She might be young, but she was cool, controlled, not in search of the inaccessible. Hadn't she told him that he wasn't her type? What, he wondered, was her type anyway?

It didn't matter. He wasn't risking anything. She wouldn't get emotionally involved with him any more than he would get emotionally involved with her. They understood one another.

'But while we're here playing truant,' he drawled huskily, 'I might see fit to limit the amount of client entertaining we do. You've never been to Paris and I know this city like the back of my hand. You're under orders to follow my lead...'

'Yes, sir!' Alice grinned. This was her big adventure and she was going to enjoy it while it lasted.

'Where did you learn to speak French?'

They sat in the sunshine outside one of the smart cafés close to the Louvre, where they had spent a couple of hours admiring the great works of art. He had been true to his word and work had been minimal for the past two days. They had entertained Francois and Marie after the deal had been officially signed, and had had lunch with another prospective client who had been charming and informative. But mostly they had made love.

She felt vibrantly, wonderfully alive. She had been living life in the slow lane and now she had been pulled into a Ferrari and was speeding up a highway, enjoying every second of the ride. It was thrilling, frightening and she was dreading the end, the brick wall at the end of the highway.

'Self-taught.' Gabriel sipped his strong coffee and looked at her, admiring the purity of her skin, the sharp fall of her hair, the fullness of her pink lips.

She was a revelation. They were lovers, but that did not impact on her ability to focus and work. They made love, but she didn't demand his constant attention. Neither did she give any hint that she intended what they had to last beyond Paris.

Which was good. In fact, it was great. They were having a no-strings-attached affair. She hadn't mentioned what exactly her type of guy was but he wasn't it. Admittedly, it irked him...

'Amazing.' Alice laughed. 'You must pick things up fast.'

'Necessity is the mother of invention,' Gabriel said drily. If only she knew...

Without the benefit of an expensive education, with his formative years spent either getting into trouble or else avoiding it, he had had to learn fast to compete once he'd got out into the big, bad world. His natural ability, talent and sheer untapped intellect had propelled him forward, but he had known from very early on he would need an edge, and that edge would be a second language. He had befriended a native Frenchman as soon as he'd hit the trading floor and had trained himself to speak only in French when they were in each other's company. He had learned to understand finance in another language, had learned the dialect of the stock exchange in French. He had earned his edge and it had come in very handy over the years.

'Meaning?'

'Meaning it's time for us to get back to the hotel. Looking at you is doing some very active things to my libido.' He drained his cup and stood up, and Alice followed suit.

This was what they were all about. She knew that just as she knew that she had done exactly what she had set out not to do: she had fallen under his spell. In London, she had seen the brilliant, inspired businessman, the man with formidable levels of energy who poured that energy into work.

But here she had seen the other man. The witty, charming, highly informative, sexy guy and she had fallen under his spell.

No, worse. With painful honesty, she knew that she had fallen in love with him. For her, this wasn't just a simple case of lust. No, this was the vast, unchartered territory of absolute love, the one-hundred percent absorption in another human being; the yearning and craving and not being able to envisage a life without them. In a perfect world, this was the sort of intense, soaring feeling that would be reciprocated. In her imperfect world, however, this was the nightmare that couldn't be contained and couldn't be ignored. Just thinking about her stupidity made her feel sick.

She had had searing sex with a guy who found her attractive but that was the end of it. She had launched herself down a one way street, had given her heart to a guy who certainly wouldn't be returning the favour, and it hurt. Gabriel Cabrera didn't do love. In fact, he didn't even do anything that remotely bordered on intimacy, or at least what *she* understood by intimacy. She hadn't failed to notice that when she asked questions he didn't want to answer, he abruptly, smilingly but very firmly, changed the subject.

The essence of the man remained hidden. That was the way he liked it, and that was something that was never going to change. How much more foolish could she have been? Against all the odds, against every scrap of common sense she possessed, she had handed over the most precious of emotions into the care of a man who would have run a mile had he but known. A wave of dizziness washed over her and she had to fight her way back to some semblance of normality.

They made it back to the hotel in record time. Dinner was going to be at one of Gabriel's favourite restaurants in Montmartre, somewhere chilled with an eclectic crowd.

It left them a couple of hours and she knew how those hours would be spent.

In his bedroom, in his bed…

She always made sure to return to her own bedroom, even in the early hours of the morning, but they always made love in his bedroom.

'I can't seem to keep my hands off you.' He pushed her

back against the closed door. 'Touch me,' he groaned. He unbuttoned his jeans and pulled down the zip to relieve the throbbing in his groin.

The touch of her cool hand as it wormed its way into his boxers was bliss, enough almost to send him over the edge.

'Let's make use of the bath…' He broke away to lead her into the bathroom, which was the last word in indulgence. A ridiculously large bath took centre stage with a walk-in shower to one side and twin sinks on the other side rested on black granite with a huge mirror behind.

He ran the bath, flinging in bath salts, and Alice watched him. He was poetry in motion and she couldn't get enough of him. He had stripped off her protective layer and the only one blessing was that he didn't realise that he had done so.

She had made sure to reveal as little about herself as he had revealed about himself, although he knew her thoughts on so many things. They had discussed literature, art, the paintings and sculptures they had seen, the food they had eaten and the wine they had drunk. They had talked about the people they watched, sitting outside and sipping coffee. They had compared notes on music. They had even talked about work and about the accountancy course she was due to embark upon.

'I can feel you watching me,' Gabriel said with a grin in his voice.

'That's because you're so egotistic. You think that every woman on the planet's watching you.'

'Ah…' He turned around, still smiling, and slowly got undressed. 'But you're the only one I care about.'

If only.

She had shed all her inhibitions in front of him. She had no idea how she was going to return to her role of perfect secretary—not when she was crazy about him, when he had seen her naked, when he had touched her in her most intimate places. But men were brilliant at detaching and she would be as well.

The water was beautifully warm and blissful. The bath was easily big enough for two and she slid between his legs, her back against his stomach, her head tucked against his neck.

He squirted some liquid soap into one hand and took his time massaging her breasts. She could feel him pressed against her, a shaft of steel, proof positive of how much she turned him on.

She sighed and slipped down lower into the water and, eyes closed, she lost herself in pure sensation as his hand moved from her breasts down over her stomach and between her thighs.

'Don't...' she protested as he found the sensitive bud and began rubbing it, eliciting broken, gasping groans.

'Don't what?'

'Stop or I'll...' Too late. Her body shuddered as she climaxed. Her breathing quickened and she cried out and turned in the water, thankfully not sending too much over the side of the bath, and she sat on him, but she knew as well as he did that without protection it was too risky.

So, instead, she did what he had done to her. Watching him climax was such a turn-on that she couldn't wait for them to get out of the bath and find the bed.

Was it her imagination or was there an urgency to their love-making that had not been there before? They would be leaving the following evening.

Gabriel could have just kept touching her, making love with her, and skipped dinner altogether but with just an hour to get ready and leave the hotel he turned to her and smiled.

'So...' he drawled, nestling her against him. They had

barely bothered to dry themselves. They had been too hungry for one another. 'We leave tomorrow.'

'We do.' Alice lowered her eyes and placed her hand flat against his hair-roughened chest.

'What do you think of Paris?'

'I think one day I'll be back. It's beautiful. I love the architecture, the art galleries, the museums… There's nothing about it I *don't* love.'

'And London? I don't think this thing we have has run its course…' He was as hot for her now as he had been on day one—as he had been even before then, if he was entirely truthful.

'Meaning?'

'Meaning, my dear secretary, that I'm not ready for our spate of truancy to come to an end.'

Alice raised clear eyes to his. *He wasn't ready for this to end.* She knew exactly what he meant—he meant that he hadn't yet grown bored with her. But he would, and when that happened she would be utterly destroyed.

More than that, having her around would begin to exasperate him. She would be just another woman to be discarded, except he would find that she was still there, still working for him, still *visible.* Would she end up buying a bouquet of goodbye flowers for herself?

'That's not how I see this panning out,' she told him and he drew apart and looked at her with a frown.

'What do you mean?' He smiled. 'We're still hot for one another. No point denying it, Alice. So you work for me and I've always had a policy of not mixing business with pleasure—but what's the saying about stable doors and a bolting horse…?'

'When we leave, Gabriel, it's over. That's what I said at the beginning and I haven't changed my mind.' Would she have responded differently if she hadn't done the unthinkable and fallen in love with him? Would she have been able to keep it as something fun and casual and then, when it was over, cheerfully return to life as she knew it?

Temptation to take that road dug into her and she fought it with the gritted determination of someone swimming upstream against a strong current.

'You don't mean that.'

She swung her legs over the side of the bed and began flinging clothes on, eyes firmly averted from his face. 'I mean every word of it, Gabriel,' she said. 'It's been amazing, but…'

Gabriel couldn't believe what he was hearing. He had never suffered rejection from any woman. He had always been the one to do the rejecting.

'But we can't keep our hands off one another!' he exploded, leaping out of the bed and snatching his boxers. He glared at her, challenging her to refute that, which she didn't. 'I don't see what the problem is!'

Fully dressed now, she at last felt strong enough to meet his glittering, bemused, demanding gaze but she still had to keep her distance.

'The problem is that we don't think alike, Gabriel. You take because you can and then, when you're bored, you move on to someone else. That's not me. I don't want to waste my time having an affair with someone unless I think it's going somewhere. Which is not the case here,' she added quickly, just in case he got it into his head that she was asking him to define what he felt for her.

'I'm just saying that we need to keep things black and white. This was a bubble. It's too late to say that it wasn't a good idea, but what's done is done, and now we can move forward and continue our working relationship and put this behind us as something enjoyable that won't be repeated.'

'I can't believe I'm hearing this,' he rasped, still incredulous. 'I've had my fair share of difficult women in my time, but you're not one of them! Or are you…?'

That cut to the quick. She was anything but, if only he knew. And thank goodness he didn't.

'I'm not,' she said shortly. 'But I'm realistic. Just like you. Except we have different realities. I want a man for life and I'm prepared to do my utmost to find him. You want a woman for two minutes and you'll never look further for anything longer.'

CHAPTER SEVEN

THEY HAD LEFT London with spring promising to be a fine one. They had returned to dank drizzle and the grey, cold weather had continued for the two weeks since they had been back.

Paris seemed like a dream. A wonderful dream to be locked away and only taken out at night, when she remembered everything—where they had gone, what they had talked about and, most of all, the heady excitement when they had made love.

She had been right to do what she had done. He had railed against her decision for five minutes, had tried to convince her that carrying on their affair was a good idea, but she hadn't failed to notice that in the end, when she had refused, he had ultimately let it go, already moving on.

And now...

She sighed and frowned at her computer, trying to focus. There wasn't a minute of the day when she wasn't aware of him. When he stood next to her to explain something, she could feel her weak, treacherous body begin to go into meltdown. Her head might try and box him up neatly but her body remembered the way it had felt under those roving hands and that exploring mouth.

He, on the other hand, seemed to have no problem with the way their working relationship had continued.

In her darker moments, she thought that he might be quietly relieved that she had made the decision that she had. It had certainly spared him the effort of having to engineer a break-up while maintaining the status quo.

The connecting door between their offices was pushed open and she tensed and looked up with a brittle, polite smile.

'I need you to book two tickets to the opera. Source me one that isn't too challenging. Best seats.'

Alice nodded. The rictus smile never left her face but something inside twisted painfully.

This was bound to happen. She had braced herself for it, for the moment when he found himself a replacement. A fortnight! What they had shared had barely been given a decent burial.

'When would you like me to book these tickets for?'

'Tonight.'

'That might be impossible, if it's one of the more popular operas.'

'Mention my name. I give generously to the Opera House. They'll find seats.' He strolled towards her and dropped a stack of files on her desk. 'And you'll have to get through these before you leave tonight.'

'But it's already five-thirty!'

'Tough.' He flicked back the cuff of his white shirt and strolled back into his office, shutting the door behind him.

Gabriel had never put himself out for any woman and he wasn't about to start now, but her cool detachment got on his nerves. It was as if Paris had never happened. She had even returned to her dreary grey garb, having tried to return the designer clothes he had ordered her to buy in Paris.

Naturally he had refused but he suspected that the whole lot had probably been given to charity. No reminders.

The worst of it was that he still wanted her. He couldn't

look at her without the memory of that slender, willowy body writhing underneath him. Another woman was what he needed, he had decided. He had had his change and it was time to return to what he knew.

He settled down to work and didn't look up until there was a knock on his door and he saw, with surprise, that it was nearly seven.

'Finished already?' he asked, swinging back in the chair and looking at her with brooding, unreadable eyes. 'Scanned and sent off everything?'

'Your date is here, Gabriel.' It was a challenge just getting the words out. So, he had reverted to type. Bethany Dawkins was small, curvaceous and dressed to impress in a figure-hugging black dress with a neckline that plunged almost to the waist, displaying bountiful breasts restrained behind a sliver of black netting. Alice had looked at the other woman and immediately felt dowdy, drab and unappealing, and she had known from the way the other woman's eyes had skimmed over her that she wasn't alone in that opinion.

She had already buzzed through to him that the tickets had been booked. She doubted sexy little Bethany with the flowing dark hair would be in the slightest bit interested in opera.

'Wonderful.' He stood up and began slinging on his jacket.

'Have a lovely evening,' she said through gritted teeth.

Gabriel paused, as though suddenly struck by an errant thought. 'With Bethany for company, I undoubtedly will. Opera interest you, Alice?'

'You know it does.' It was the first time she had alluded to one of the many conversations they had had over a bottle of wine before they'd had to return to the hotel, like adolescents unable to go long without touching one another.

'Of course. I'd forgotten. Care to join us? I'm sure it would be possible to have them arrange for a third seat to be made available.'

And witness first hand how easily he had moved on? Watch them holding hands and staring at each other in that 'can't wait to climb into bed after this' way? That was how he had looked at her in Paris. Over meals, in the back seat of the limo, he had looked at her with dark hunger, as though the time couldn't go by fast enough until he was in bed with her again.

'I'll give that a miss. Thank you. And, to answer your question about the files, yes, everything's been done so, if it's all the same with you, I'll leave now. I shall be going to visit my mother in Devon tomorrow and I thought I might stay over until Tuesday. I could look in on that customer we've been having problems with in Exeter. It's no trouble and it'll save you having to make the trip yourself.'

'How far does your mother live from Exeter?'

'Close enough.' Something else that he'd forgotten. She had told him the name of the little village where her mother lived, although she had kept all other surplus information to herself. Had he forgotten *everything* she had said to him? He had appeared so attentive, but had it been in one ear and out the other?

Well, he certainly had form when it came to that, she thought bitterly, but it hurt, because she had been one-hundred percent committed when she had talked to him.

'I think your hot date might be getting a bit impatient outside,' she reminded him coolly.

'And that's a problem because…?' He wondered why the sudden disappearing act for a long weekend. Since she had effectively walked out on him, he had been thinking about her non-stop, which alternately baffled and angered him— hence his decision to seek some replacement therapy. But not even the delectable woman waiting for him outside could kill the curiosity he felt when it came to Alice.

He knew that she visited her mother every weekend and, for the life of him, that seemed peculiar. It took filial devotion to whole new lengths.

And this weekend, she wanted to stay longer. He knew that the village was only forty-five minutes' drive from his client, so why the pressing urgency to stay the day?

Did she visit more than just her mother when she vanished on those mysterious trips to the back of beyond? The more he considered that option, the more likely it seemed, and of course there could be only one pressing reason for her to trek all the way down there every weekend without fail. A man.

She had slept with him and she had fancied the hell out of him, or so he had thought. Frankly, wasn't it a little suspect that she could move from fancying him to treating him like a complete stranger within a matter of hours? Women didn't operate like that. Detachment did not come as second nature to them. Why would Alice be the exception to the rule? It was as though the woman she had been in Paris had stayed there.

He had never been given to flights of imagination. He had always considered that the luxury of people who had too much spare time on their hands, but he was discovering that his imagination was playing all sorts of games now as he stood there, looking at her.

So, she had slept with him. Was it because the guy she really wanted was not available? Was the man married? Was that what those weekend visits were all about? Was it a so-called duty visit to dear mama, but really to hook up with some sleazy guy with a wife and kids who gave her sex now and again while promising to leave his albatross family one day?

Red mist settled over his eyes. 'I'll expect you back here first thing on Monday. Harrisons can wait. There's too much work here for you to take a day off.'

'I've already booked the day off,' Alice told him abruptly. 'I was being helpful when I suggested I visit Harrisons—it would actually have cut into my day. But they're only a hop and a skip away and I shall probably be in the area to do some…shopping anyway. I don't mind popping in and picking up the hard copy information we need.' *How dared he think that he could be heavy handed with her just because he had moved on and was involved with someone else?*

Just then Bethany appeared at the door, her face a picture of petulance. He had met Bethany several months ago at a company do. Her father—an Argentinian man in his late fifties whose company had surfaced on Gabriel's radar for acquisition—had brought her along in the absence of his wife, who'd been on a cruise with a gaggle of her friends, he had told Gabriel. Bethany had visibly blossomed the second she had set eyes on Gabriel and had followed him around for the evening, much to her father's delight. She was thirty, sexy as hell and, she'd confessed with a sultry little smile, bored out of her mind with all the dreary people talking about work.

Gabriel had taken her number, vaguely intimated that he might give her a call and promptly forgotten her existence, of which he had been reminded several times in the intervening months.

He had finally, two days previously, decided to take her up on her repeated offers. This was his comfort zone— being chased by women. His comfort zone was not one in which he pursued and was knocked back.

He looked between the women and the differences could not have been more startling.

Alice was nearly six inches taller in flats, slim, with her hair neatly tied back and her pale face intelligent and attractive rather than flamboyantly beautiful. She had a composure and a stillness that the much shorter, sexier woman lacked and Gabriel stifled his irritation at finding himself losing interest in his hot date for the evening.

'Have a really nice evening.' Alice couldn't bear to see them together, to see her replacement who was everything she was not. She hated the thought that she had been the temporary aberration, and she wondered whether Gabriel had been drawn to her because she was so unlike the women he went out with as a rule.

Bethany had lost interest in Alice altogether and was preening for Gabriel's benefit, smoothing her hands over her figure-hugging dress and then twirling round, demanding to know what he thought of her outfit.

Alice turned away, not wanting to see the rampant male appreciation in his eyes, appreciation that she had once seen directed at her.

'I'll leave you to it, shall I?' She interrupted the love birds and Gabriel turned to look at her.

'If you don't mind.' His voice was ultra-polite, his eyes flat and unreadable. 'And, Alice, have a good weekend... visiting your mother...'

Alice reddened. 'I happen to have other things planned,' she muttered, because he had made her sound sad and pathetic, and he had done it on purpose. Or maybe he hadn't. Maybe he had just pushed her back into the 'efficient secretary without a life' box whose weekend occupation was visiting her mother. Not that he knew the full story behind those visits.

'Oh? Anything exciting?' Gabriel's ears pricked up. Bethany's arm possessively linking his felt like a dead

weight and it was all he could do not to shrug it off impatiently off impatiently.

'Oh, just seeing one or two people,' Alice told him
vaguely. 'You know…'

Gabriel didn't know and the not knowing preyed on
his mind for the remainder of the evening. He was irritated with his date, and then further irritated with himself, because before Paris Bethany would have been just
the thing to relieve him of whatever stress he might have
been having.

She had no interest in what was happening on the stage
and several times asked him what the plot was. She spent
quite a bit of time peering round her to see if she could
recognise anyone, and was visibly relieved when the ordeal was at an end and they could get something to eat.
Although, she said with a little moue, she really, *really,*
would have loved to have something to eat at his place.

Sex was not going to happen.

In fact, nothing was going to happen.

Gabriel fed her, listened to her while his mind drifted
in other, less welcome directions and then settled her into
his chauffeur-driven car, made his excuses and headed
back alone to his house.

So much for his attempts at distracting himself! The
only thing on his mind was Alice's remark about having
people to see at the weekend. The thought of her having a
man down there had lodged in his head, utterly destroying
the self-assurance he wore like a mantel on his shoulders.

There was no getting round it—if he had been used, if
he had been some kind of sick substitute for a man who
couldn't commit to her, then he had a right to know.

He knew where her mother lived. She had touched upon
that topic in passing, had mentioned the house with a wist-
ful smile on her face. She had talked about the little vil-

lage and the picturesque country road which she was fond
of walking down, breathing in the fragrance of the summer blossoms, the sharpness of the wintry air, dawdling
in autumn on her way from house to village to appreciate
the russet reds of the falling leaves.

Oh yes, he had a memory like a computer, and he hadn't
forgotten a single thing she had told him in Paris when
she had let her guard down and confided, told him snippets of her past which had seemed to slip out in between
their conversations about art and culture, work and deals,
the state of the world.

Alice, he thought with a frown as he retired for bed
much later that night, would have appreciated the opera.
She wouldn't have asked a bunch of idiotic questions, she
wouldn't have stifled yawns and she wouldn't have kept
looking around her like a bored kid at an adult gathering.

It all came back to Alice. He had never been this ob-
sessed with a woman and he wondered whether it was
because he still felt that they had unfinished business between them. If there was some mystery man in the background, then the business would be finished and she
would be out on her ear looking for a new job. But if there
wasn't... Maybe what they had started in Paris needed to
reach a natural conclusion.

She might say that she didn't want that, but he did.
Badly...and he was a man who always got what he wanted.

Alice finished preparing the supper and went to join her
mother in the little sitting room that overlooked the tidy,
pretty garden in which Pamela Morgan spent so much of
her spare time, pottering and enjoying being outside where
her phobia could not get a grip and drive her back to the
safety of the four walls.

There was something that her mother was keeping from

her and that was worrying. True, she would be seeing
her mother's therapist on Monday morning first thing,
but she couldn't help wondering if there had been some
sort of setback.

The sitting room was bright and airy and very different
from the sitting room in the house in which she had grown
up. Here, photos of her as a girl were proudly displayed
on the mantelpiece and the sofa and chairs were deep and
comfortable. It was a cluttered room, which was something
her father had loathed, preferring to have as few reminders
as possible around that he was a family man.

'You were telling me all about your trip to Paris,' Pamela Morgan encouraged as soon as her daughter was
sitting down, legs tucked underneath her, cosy and comfortable in her faded jogging bottoms and bedroom slippers, with her hair in a stubby ponytail.

Actually, Alice thought that talking about her trip to
Paris was pretty much all she had done since she had arrived. It had been the same last weekend and, whilst she
had done her best to skirt round the topic of Gabriel, she
had found herself talking about him, recounting some of
the anecdotes he had told her. Her mother had made a very
good listener, hardly interrupting, and Alice wondered if
she had confided more than she should have.

But if her mother wanted to hear more about the Louvre and what they had seen, or the Jardin des Tuileries and
how beautiful it was, then so be it.

Alice was accustomed to handling Pamela Morgan with
kid gloves. She tiptoed around anything too intrusive, permanently aware that her mother was not one of life's more
robust specimens.

Outside, the day had been surprisingly warm and sunny,
and the sun was only now beginning to dip, throwing the
garden into lovely, semi-sunlit relief.

In the kitchen, some meat sauce was simmering on the stove. Later they would eat together and, as always, it would be an early night.

As she chatted, her mind played with the thought of Gabriel and how he was enjoying his weekend with the pocket brunette. Had the opera been an aperitif, the taster course before the main meal? Of course it had, she chided herself scornfully. The main meal would have been the bedroom. Gabriel might be lazy when it came to every single form of emotional involvement, but he was just the opposite when it came to physical involvement. On that level, he was one-hundred percent active and engaged.

She wished she could eliminate him from her head, somehow press *delete* and get rid of all the inconvenient memories that were making her life a living hell.

She didn't want to quit her job but that was becoming a very real possibility with each passing day. Yesterday, seeing that woman in the office, had been the worst...

It was a reminder of how fleeting she had been for him. Her voice trailed off and she caught her mother looking at her speculatively; she grinned and tried to remember what she had been talking about. Paris? Work? Her flat-mate Lucy's new boyfriend?

'You're a million miles away,' Pamela said softly. 'Have been since you returned from Paris. It's not your boss, is it? He seems to have made quite an impact on you.'

Appalled, Alice's mouth dropped open and she blushed. 'Of course not!' she denied vigorously. 'I wouldn't be so stupid! You know how I feel about the whole relationship thing, Mum, after...'

'I know, dear. After your father and that dreadful boyfriend you had. But...' There was a tentative silence and then Alice was startled when her mother said quietly, 'You can't let those experiences dictate your future.'

'I—I wouldn't *do* that,' Alice stuttered. 'It's just that you have to be careful when it comes to getting involved. It's all too easy to make the wrong choices!' She continued with heated earnestness, 'I will make very sure that, if and when I become *seriously* involved with a guy, he'll be someone who is right for me! Honestly, Mum, you want to meet my boss! He has a constantly revolving carousel of women who service his needs and, then, pouf! They're gone, straight through the exit, and ten seconds later another version is heading in his direction. He plucks them off the carousel the way someone plucks fruit from a tree! Has a little taste and then chucks what's left!'

'You're far too young to be so cynical about men...'

Alice bit her tongue but she and her mother knew each other well and she looked away because she could read what her mother was thinking.

If you're not careful you'll end up with no one because no one will fit the bill.

'I'd rather be on my own than make a mistake,' she said, her cheeks bright red, pre-empting the statement before it could be made.

Her mother sighed and lowered her eyes. She was not argumentative, and neither was Alice, but she had to be firm. She'd always had to look out for the two of them and it somehow felt treacherous for her mother to tell her that she was too cynical about men.

'What's the point of learning curves if you don't learn from them?' Fat lot of good that had done for her, she thought. She had been swept up in the same tidal wave of lust and desire that afflicted all the women who came into Gabriel's magical range. And she hadn't stopped at the lust and desire, which would have been bad enough. Oh no, she had taken it a step further and fallen in love with the man!

Her mother would have been distraught, had she only

known. Like her, Pamela Morgan had worked hard to cultivate a healthy scepticism when it came to the opposite sex. There was nothing wrong with that. It was called reality. How many times had they joked that men were more trouble than they were worth? For her mother, it would have been more than just a joke.

They usually ate in the kitchen, unless there was something on the telly they both wanted to watch, in which case trays were brought—although her mother never failed to complain that eating in front of the television was a sloppy habit.

But her mother watched a great deal of television and there had been times when some detective series or gardening show had been too tempting to miss.

Tonight, Alice set the table for them, leaving her mother in the sitting room, where she was happily flicking between her crossword book and the television.

She had almost had an argument with her mother and she felt awful about that.

Not only was the man intruding into all her thoughts, her waking moments, her dreams, but he was now managing to interrupt the easy flow of conversation with her mother.

She slammed place mats on the table and was reaching for wine glasses when there was a knock at the door.

Everyone used the kitchen door, but whoever it was had banged on the front door and, after just a brief hesitation, she dropped what she was doing and arrived at the front door at exactly the same time as her mother.

'You sit back down,' Alice said firmly. 'I'll get rid of whoever is out there.'

'No! I mean, dear, I'll get this. I don't like just telling people to go away. You know—it's a small village and I wouldn't want to get a reputation for being the sort of person who can't be polite to visitors...'

'Mum, if it's a visitor, of course I'm not going to send them on their merry way! But if it's someone trying to sell double glazing…'

'I'm not sure they do that any more, dear. Do they?'

As they stood there, vaguely quibbling, there was another loud knock on the door and, with a sigh of exasperation, Alice pulled open the front door and stared…

'What are *you* doing here?' Her mother was right behind her and she edged out of the door and half-shut it behind her, then she poked her head through and told her mother, who was avid with curiosity, that the caller was for her.

'Who is it?'

'No one! You…er…go inside and I'll be in, literally in a minute or two…' For a moment, Alice thought that her mother was about to ignore that suggestion but, after a brief staring match, Pamela Morgan tutted and headed towards the kitchen, not before casting another curious glance in the direction of the front door.

'What do you want? What are you doing here?'

Gabriel stared down at Alice. This was an Alice he had not seen before. Not the brisk, efficient secretary in the neat, uninspiring suit, or the glamorous, leggy woman in the designer clothes she had bought when she had been in Paris with him. A beautiful, fresh-faced girl who looked her age, with a ponytail and wearing stay-at-home, faded clothes and peculiar bedroom slippers with a cartoon motif.

Warmer weather had brought out a band of light freckles across the bridge of her nose. He had completely forgotten why he had come but he was damn glad that he had. Just seeing her did something to him and he fidgeted and looked away before resting his gaze once again on her upturned face.

'I couldn't get you out of my head.' Hell, had he just *said that*?

'What?' Alice was so shocked by that statement that her mouth fell open. Her eyes were glued to his face, which the early evening threw into shadow. He looked tired and dishevelled and drop-dead gorgeous. He had pushed up the arms of his long-sleeved cotton jumper and the sprinkling of dark hair brought back vivid memories of those strong arms around her. His low-slung jeans clung to him, delineating his long, muscular legs.

She felt her nipples pushing in anticipation against her bra, wanting to be touched and teased and licked.

'Shouldn't you be with…that woman who came to the office yesterday?' Alice asked huskily and Gabriel delivered a slow, amused smile that rocked her to the core.

Alice stared down at her feet. The pulse in her neck was beating fast and here, in these clothes, she had that weird, out-of-body feeling that she had had in Paris when she had thrown caution to the winds and jumped into bed with him.

He was making her aware of something better out there, something wild and free, and she *hated* him for that because she knew that it was all an illusion.

'It turns out that she didn't do it for me.' Gabriel had made a decision; it was one that had come to him when she had pulled open the front door and he had looked at her.

He was done telling himself that he was not built for pursuit. He was done pretending that he wasn't jealous whenever he thought of her with another man. If these reactions stemmed from the fact that what they had hadn't run its course, then it was up to him to ensure that it did run its course. How else was he going to get her out of his system?

'Are you going to invite me into the house?'

'No. You shouldn't be here, Gabriel.' But she was light with relief that the pocket-sized brunette hadn't become her replacement. It was stupid and it was cowardly but she couldn't help it.

'I know I shouldn't.' He raked his fingers through his hair, not too sure where he went from here.

Alice looked at him, perplexed.

'Is there a man in there?' he questioned suddenly, roughly, and Alice's mouth tightened with outrage.

'I'm not you, Gabriel. I don't hop from one bed to another without pausing for breath.'

'I didn't hop anywhere with Bethany. I put her in my car and my driver took her back to her house. End of story.'

'Just go, Gabriel.' She sighed and stared to the side of him, but his image was imprinted so forcibly in her head that every bit of him had been committed to memory. He was in her system like a virus which she couldn't budge.

'I'm not going anywhere.'

'Why? Why? I've told you…'

'Let me in.'

'You always think that you can get whatever you want.'

Gabriel stared at her and she squirmed under his unrelenting dark gaze. What would she do if he kissed her right now? Melt. She was melting now, liquid heat gathering between her legs, dampening her underwear. *He couldn't get her out of his head.* She told herself that those were just meaningless words, but they bounced around in her head until she was giddy.

'Let me in.'

He was as immovable as the rock of Gibraltar, standing there in all his brooding, intense glory, and with a little sigh of resignation Alice stood aside.

Her mother was hovering in the kitchen and introductions were made. Pamela Morgan launched into a series of questions, her curiosity on red alert, and Alice groaned silently to herself. If she had never said a word about Gabriel, she might have been able to channel him out of the house without too much difficulty—as just her boss who happened to be down to see a client and had popped in for…reasons best known to himself.

But she had spent far too much time telling her mother about him, describing him, inviting the curiosity that was now unstoppable.

How great to finally meet the man her daughter worked for! 'You never told me that he was so good-looking!'… 'My daughter loves her job; I can tell because she talks so much about it!'… 'And Paris…how wonderful that she had the opportunity to go there! She can't stop talking about it!'

'You *asked* me, Mum!' Alice avoided eye contact with Gabriel but she could feel him simmering with his own curiosity. 'I talked about Paris because *you asked me*!'

Her mother had chosen, however, to skirt round that technicality.

'I've intruded,' Gabriel murmured. Pamela Morgan was an attractive woman, with a frailty that her daughter lacked. Not even the loose-fitting dress or the long, cream cardigan could conceal her good looks. Was that why her daughter was so self-conscious about her appearance? Was there some sort of unspoken rivalry between mother and daughter? And, yet, no; there was clearly a strong bond there.

This was the first time he had ever met any relative of any woman he had slept with, aside from Bethany's father. Meeting the family had been something he had always heavily discouraged. Now, he was intensely curious, intensely curious to join the dots and make connections— intensely, inexplicably curious just to find out more.

'You're not intruding! Is he, Alice?'

'Well, now that you mention it…' She caught Gabriel's eye and noted the wicked gleam of amusement.

'That's very kind…may I call you Pamela? Yes? Well, you're very kind, but I won't be staying long.'

'Yes.' Alice stood up with a wide, false smile. 'Gabriel has to be on his way. Don't you, Gabriel? He's probably got all sorts of plans for the evening.'

'None,' Gabriel drawled. He settled down comfortably in the kitchen chair to which he had been ushered. 'But I will have, if you ladies would allow me to take you both out for a meal…?' His sharp eyes noted the quick look that was exchanged, and then Pamela Morgan was on her feet, clutching her cardigan tightly around her.

'You two go out. There's a lovely little restaurant in the village, just opened…'

'There is?' Alice gaped. 'And, no! We won't be going anywhere!' She glared at Gabriel who returned the glare with a comfortable smile of satisfaction.

'Yes, you will, Alice! I insist. We eat in every single weekend. It will do you good to get out and see the place for a change. Plus, there's food here for me, and what's left over I can pop in the freezer. And the weather is so nice at the moment. Such a lovely change from all that rain we've been having. Alice, darling, why don't you go and change, and you two young things can go out and have some fun.'

'Mum…'

'If you're sure, Pamela…' Gabriel stood up, exuding innate charm. 'Why don't you run along, Alice? Change into your glad rags? And, in the meantime, Pamela and I can get to know one another…'

CHAPTER EIGHT

ALICE FUMED. WHY had he shown up on her doorstep? It was utterly out of character for him, but then being dumped was out of character for him as well. Was that why he had said that he couldn't get her out of his head? Once you stripped that remark down to its bare bones, what you were left with was a man who wanted something of which he had been deprived, whatever the cost.

He was impossible!

She had practically nothing to wear. She didn't come down to Devon intent on having nights out. Her wardrobe consisted of comfortable clothes to hang around the house in. With a groan of despair, she rummaged through the bottom shelves where clothes from another era had been shoved and forgotten.

Gabriel here, in her mother's house, felt like an invasion of her privacy. He was seeing where she had lived for years; seeing the photos of her which were liberally scattered throughout the small house; the little drawings she had done which her mother had kept in a box during those long, miserable years when she'd been married, drawings which she'd had framed as soon as she had a house of her own.

He was a billionaire and she couldn't help wondering what he thought of her mother's house: too small, not smart

enough, filled with mementoes and knickknacks that had
cost practically nothing. Everything else, the more expensive stuff, had been sold off when her father had died
and the family home sold. Her mother had not wanted to
bring any bad memories with her to wherever she chose
to put down roots.

Alice wasn't at all ashamed of where she had lived but it
was only human to see your own particular circumstances
through the eyes of someone else. In this case, her arrogant, super-rich boss.

She looked around her own bedroom with critical eyes.
Nothing had been done to it since she had moved out. It
was in good condition, but dated. The wallpaper was old-
style floral and the bed and the dressing table harked back
to a different era—the era of cheap reproduction furniture
that was functional but lacking in style. It had served its
purpose and, for the first time, Alice was slightly ashamed
that she had not encouraged her mother to do some basic
renovations to the house.

Yes, some of what she earned went on paying her mother's therapist, but there was always enough left over to
spend a little on the house.

Her mother, whilst she probably would have been able
to afford some of those renovations, would have swept
aside the suggestion as being a waste of money. That,
like so much else, was a legacy of her past, unhappy life,
where money had never been thrown around and where
the housekeeping had been frugal.

Eager to get downstairs and curtail whatever conversation Gabriel was having with her mother, Alice showered and changed as fast as she could. The black trousers,
which had been folded on the bottom shelf, thankfully still
fit; the red jumper might be baggy but its colour had not
been diminished in the wash, and at least it looked jollier

than the greys, blacks and dark blues that comprised most of the rest of the wardrobe of clothes.

As an afterthought, she applied a light covering of make-up—some mascara, a little blush, some lip gloss.

I couldn't get you out of my head...

She could feel his remark burning a hole through all her defences, worming its way past her conviction that it was just another example of his arrogance, and she groaned again.

She barged into the kitchen to find Gabriel enjoying a cup of tea and her mother giggling. Giggling! They both looked up as she entered, like a couple of kids found out in a conspiracy. Alice took a few deep breaths, gathering herself and resisting the urge to ask them what, exactly, what so funny.

She had been gone less than forty minutes and they had become best friends!

'This is all I could find to wear,' she said ungraciously, and was treated to a wolfish smile from Gabriel.

'You look lovely, dear. Doesn't she look lovely, Gabriel? You should wear red more often. It suits you.'

'It certainly does...' he murmured. 'We're going to an Italian restaurant. Your favourite type of food.'

Pamela looked between them with keen interest. 'How do you know that?' she asked with, Alice thought, a complete lack of tact.

'Oh, I know a great many things about your daughter, Pamela...'

'Because,' Alice snapped, 'when you're stuck in someone's company for days on end, you tend to find out superficial things about them. Like what their favourite cuisine is.'

'*Stuck in my company?* I got the impression that you rather—'

'Okay,' Alice interrupted hurriedly, before something was said that would have her mother's curiosity spiked even more than it already was. 'Shall we go? I don't want to be long, because…'

'Where will you be staying, Gabriel?'

Gabriel shrugged. 'Well, I hadn't thought ahead.'

'You'll save some money if you stay here. The spare bedroom is small but it's tidy. I use it as a sewing room, but I could just pop my bits and bobs in my sewing box.'

'Gabriel doesn't need to save money, Mum. And I'm sure he won't be staying overnight.'

'It's way too late for me to drive back to London,' Gabriel said thoughtfully. 'And don't we all need to save money?'

Alice controlled hysterical laughter. This was the man who travelled first class and only stayed in the finest five-star hotels. She doubted the concept of *saving money* had ever crossed his radar.

'It would be rude of me to turn down such a kind invitation.' He smiled at Pamela, the sort of smile that would have had any woman on the planet eating out of his hands.

'No,' Alice inserted firmly. 'If you really can't drive back tonight, then I'm sure we can fix you up with a pleasant local hotel. Closer to Exeter, of course, because I'm sure you'll want to visit Harrisons first thing Monday…'

'Of course you must stay here, Gabriel. I've never seen my daughter as happy and as fulfilled as she has been since she's started working for you. And if in return you want to buy me a new toaster, well, then it would be downright churlish of me to refuse…'

With which, she shooed them both out of the house.

Head held high, Alice snatched her jacket from the coat hook by the front door and stormed out into the cool darkness. She closed her ears to the friendly banter between

Gabriel and her mother and, when the front door had been quietly but firmly shut on them, she turned to him, hands on her hips.

'How dare you?'

'How dare I what?' He guided her towards his black SUV, which had made light work of the journey down.

'Become best friends with my mother!'

'You're being ridiculous.' He opened the passenger door and steered her into the car.

'I am *not* being ridiculous!' she hissed as soon as he was behind the wheel, starting the engine into throaty life. 'You shouldn't have come here.'

'Don't tell me you're not glad…no, *excited*…that I'm here. I can *feel* it.'

'I am *not*…'

Whatever she had been about to say was lost as his mouth hit hers in a crushing, hungry kiss, a kiss he had been waiting for ever since they had returned from Paris and taken up the charade of playing boss-secretary as though nothing had happened between them.

Hand behind the nape of her neck, he pulled her towards him and carried on kissing her, their tongues melding, their bodies yearning for one another.

Alice was giddy from the fierceness of her driven response. Her fingers curled into his hair and she moaned with a mixture of wanting and not wanting, unable to help herself, and hating herself for her weakness.

Finally, he drew back and looked at her.

'Don't spin me any yarns about not wanting me,' he growled. 'If I were to take you right here, right now, you wouldn't run screaming from this car. In fact, you'd get that sexy body of yours in all the right positions to have me in you!'

'That's not—'

'It damn well is! Stop running away from the obvious!'

'I never said you weren't an attractive man!' Her lips tingled from where they had been ravished. Her whole body tingled. He was right, he could have her in a heart-beat, and it was a shaming thought. She had spent the past two weeks fighting to maintain a controlled front and in a few seconds he had demolished it like a house of cards. She wanted to sob from frustration.

Gabriel smiled and turned his attention to the road. 'So...' He guided the car along the narrow road that led to the village. 'You've never been happier than you are now, working for me. Apparently, I'm an exciting boss.'

'Is that what my mother told you?'

'She's not what I had expected. Somehow I had it in my head that she was more like you.'

'Meaning what, Gabriel?'

'Meaning...strong, focused, opinionated. She's a beau-tiful woman, Alice, but she seems to live on her nerves.'

'I don't like you prying into my personal life.' But her voice was defeated. He had crossed the last frontier. In the space of a few weeks, she had gone from being the cool, together secretary he had taken on to replace his string of inept temps to a woman who had fallen under his spell, slept with him and now...the woman whose entire life would be laid bare.

'I'm expressing interest, Alice,' he said gently. 'Not prying.'

'I never asked for your interest.' She rested her head against the leather head-rest and stared through the win-dow at the blurred, dark countryside racing past her. In a few minutes, they would be in the village. They could actually have walked. On a nice evening, it was a joy to stroll down the country lanes, breathing in the fragrance of the trees and flowers. It was a thirty-minute walk that she had always found therapeutic.

Sure enough, the village twinkled ahead of them, and he found his way easily to the village square, where he parked the car and then killed the engine.

He looked at her for a while. She had the most riveting face he had ever seen, even when that face was turned away from him. He wanted to drag her back into his arms, kiss her all over again, force her out of her coolness, which was unbearable now that he had seen another side to her.

He was baffled by the strength of his reactions to her. He wasn't just in hot, determined pursuit; he wanted more from her than just her body and her compliance. He had never been remotely interested in any of his past lovers' backgrounds or in trying to make sense of them.

He had taken what had been on offer and looked no further. Yes, so he had been lazy. He wasn't lazy now.

'Why is your mother hesitant about telling you that she has a boyfriend?'

Alice's head whipped round and she looked at him, shocked by what he had just said. 'Don't be ridiculous! You don't know what you're talking about. And I resent you poking your nose into my life, Gabriel!' She yanked open the car door and sprang out of the car, wildly looking round for whatever Italian restaurant they were going to. It wouldn't be hard to find. It wasn't as though the village was bursting at the seams with chichi eating places.

It took her two seconds to spot the red-and-white-checked awning where, from memory, a corner shop used to be, tucked away on the corner and easy to miss, if it hadn't been for the bright lights and the people inside.

'Don't run away from me!'

His hand snapped out, holding her firmly in place before she could flee to the safety of the crowded restaurant.

'I'm not running away!' No. She wasn't. She was staring up into those deep, dark eyes and bitterly resenting his presence here in her treasured, private territory. 'What did you mean when you said that…that mum had a boyfriend?'

Gabriel felt some of the tension leave him. She had kissed him. Hell, she had kissed him as hungrily as he had kissed her. And then, almost immediately, she had pushed him away. At least she wasn't pushing him away now. It was something.

'I'll tell you over dinner. I take it that's the restaurant over there?' He began walking, pointedly not tucking her arm into his, although he wanted to.

This, Alice thought, was what lust felt like. In Paris, when they had been playing truant, when she had fallen madly and stupidly in love with him, he had shown affection in all sorts of small ways: holding hands, turning to kiss her, reaching out to tuck her hair behind her ear when the breeze was whipping it across her face…

But they weren't playing truant now. They were back in England, and it was pretty clear that he might still want her, but those gestures of affection were no longer appropriate. His hands were very firmly in his jacket pockets and he was barely glancing in her direction as they walked briskly over to the restaurant.

'So, tell me,' Alice reluctantly demanded, once they were tucked away in the corner of the restaurant with two over-sized menus in front of them and a bottle of white wine on the way.

'I'm sorry if I said something you would rather not have heard,' Gabriel told her roughly. 'This wasn't a long, soul-searching conversation with your mother, Alice. She mentioned in passing that there was a man interested in her, someone she had started seeing recently, and then she laughed nervously and told me that she was working up the courage to tell you about him.'

Alice felt the sting of hurt prick the back of her eyes. She was lost for words. Her mother had given no indication of any boyfriend lurking backstage but then again, she thought with painful honesty, when was the last time she had encouraged confidences of that nature? No, she had held forth on men and the need to be careful with them; she had talked long and hard about them both learning from experience; she had bitterly and often harked back to her feckless father as a learning curve her mother should never forget...

That had never been fertile ground for her mother to tell her that she was involved with a man.

'I see.' Her face was stiff with the effort of trying not to cry. She wished he wouldn't be gentle with her. She wished he would just be the single-minded bastard who only wanted one thing, whatever the cost. She stiffened as he reached across the table and laid his hand over hers.

'I told her that I was sure you would be delighted to know that she had found someone, a companion...' Because, for all her assertiveness, her spikiness, her boundless ability to speak whatever was on her mind and suffer the consequences, she had a big heart.

How did he know that? He just did.

'Maybe I wouldn't have been *that* delighted.' She pulled her hand out from under his, instantly missing the warmth that had passed between them, and smiled at the waiter as he dribbled wine into Gabriel's glass and went through the performance of asking whether it was all right.

As soon as her glass had been poured, she drank it and looked to Gabriel for a refill.

'What do you mean?'

Alice threw the last of her privacy through the window.

He had made so many inroads into her life that there didn't seem much point hanging on to it. Fortified by the wine, she sighed and traced a little pattern on her empty white plate. Then she looked at him.

'I'm afraid my childhood wasn't a happy one,' she said heavily. 'My father was...a bully and a philanderer. I grew up having to deal with the effect that had on Mum. You're right—she's not like me. She's always been frail. You know...?' She darted a quick look at him, watching to see if he was repelled at what she was telling him, and then melting because his expression was so sympathetic. 'I can't believe I'm telling you this. I...I'm not usually the sort of person who confides.'

'You've grown up being strong for the sake of your mother.' Gabriel sipped his wine and impatiently brushed aside the waiter who was approaching them for their order.

So this was what it felt like, he thought, to involve yourself in someone else's life story. His lifetime had been spent as a solitary figure, forging his own destiny, never needing input from anyone else because experience had taught him that other people's input was always largely self-serving. He had grown up fighting his own battles single-handed and then, when the battles had been fought, reaping the reward without bothering to search any deeper. It was a formula that had always worked for him.

And still did, he reminded himself a little too vigorously, before he allowed pointless sentimentality to cloud the issue.

'When my father died, my mother was free to build a life of her own, but she had been damaged by years of having to put up with his selfishness. She became more and more anxious and now...' Alice shrugged her shoulders expressively. 'Over time she became fearful of leaving the house. It's been quite bad. In fact, I've had to hire a therapist to try and work some magic…and it's working. She's been out more in the last few months than ever before. Small steps. But I guess I've been guilty of laying it on thick about not getting involved with another man. I never said so out loud…' *But she had given that impression.* 'Who is this guy, anyway?'

'I don't know the details, Alice. Like I said, it was a fleeting conversation.'

'Whilst you were busy charming her, you mean.' Her retort was half-hearted. 'I wondered how she knew about this restaurant. I guess they must have come here, which is terrific, because it means she's getting out of the house, beginning to build a normal life for herself.'

And in the meantime, Alice wondered, how normal was *her* life? She had been so busy making sure they both learned valuable lessons about the nature of men that she had forgotten how young she still was. And her mother *had* tried to remind her of that, but she had unhelpfully brushed aside those conversations.

'So there you have it,' she said crisply. 'It would have been better if you hadn't known, but…'

'Why?'

'Why?' Alice laughed and there was an edge to her laughter. 'Because you're not interested in other people's lives, Gabriel. You're probably embarrassed that you've ended up here with me pouring all this out, but it's your fault for showing up unannounced.'

'Ah, we're back to the Alice Morgan who wants to pick a fight with me… It's not going to work.'

She was sorely tempted to ask him about *his* personal life but something held her back. Maybe she didn't want to hear that mantra about never committing to any woman. Maybe she wanted to believe that…that *what?*

That she could somehow change him because she was in love with him?

Hell would freeze over before that happened!

But, as they ordered food, she was keenly aware that she had let all her guard down with him, that the chance of returning to the fragile relationship she had worked hard to put back in place after Paris was changed for good.

And, for her part, she had seen yet another slice of this complex man—a genuinely thoughtful side that he kept well hidden under an armour of a ruthless, single-minded drive to succeed.

She ruefully thought that, while she had been busy never taking chances, while she had made a big deal of her non-relationship with Alan as yet further proof of how important it was to protect yourself from being hurt, her mother, for all her problems and her devastating marriage, had been courageous enough to take chances of her own.

The only chances Alice had taken were those snatched days and nights in Paris when she had thrown caution to the winds and had allowed her body to rule her head.

And she had made damn sure to scuttle back to the safety of what she knew the second they had returned to London.

From under lowered lashes, she watched as he worked his way through his food, the way he engaged her in conversation whether she wanted him to or not, the tactful way he desisted from prying further into her past. She took in those long, brown fingers curled around the stem of his wine glass as he sipped his wine and the brooding intensity of his dark eyes as they rested on her flushed face...

Sensitive to every nuance of her body language, Gabriel sensed the shift in atmosphere.

He had stopped being the enemy she had mistakenly

slept with, the enemy whose hot kisses she wanted to resist but couldn't...

He had her and satisfaction roared through him. He
had stopped thinking that he just needed to sleep with
her to get her out of his system. He now thought that he
just needed to sleep with her. He needed to have her body
under him, on him and alongside him. He needed to feel
the silky smoothness of her slender thighs between his
legs. He needed to touch her breasts and feel her melt
under his hands.

The meal couldn't end soon enough for him, although
he didn't think he could actually sleep with her in her
mother's house. Thinking about having to wait until they
were back in London brought a painful ache in his groin.
He could barely focus on the conversation she was having with him.

'If you'd rather I stay somewhere else overnight,' he
told her gruffly, 'then I'm happy to oblige.'

'What makes you say that?'

'The fact that you tried so hard to dissuade your mother
from her hospitality.'

'I've never known my mum to dig her heels in the way
she did,' Alice confessed, closing her knife and fork on
what had been a superb meal. 'But, no.' She shot him a
flushed, determined stare and her heart picked up speed
as he met her gaze and held it for longer than was necessary. 'She would be upset if you disappeared to stay in a
bed and breakfast. In fact, she would probably blame *me*.
She probably blames me for trying to over-protect her.'
The admission was forced out of her and she lowered her
eyes. 'If I hadn't been so...forceful, who knows? She might
have found Mr Right a bit sooner.'

'He may not be Mr Right,' Gabriel told her gently. 'But
he might just be the guy who takes her out of herself,

someone she's willing to have fun with even if it doesn't
last the course...'

'What are you trying to say?'

'It's better to feel something, anything, rather than hide
behind a wall in the hope that you don't end up getting
hurt.' He was uncomfortably aware that this was advice
he didn't actually follow to the letter himself, although
his lack of emotional involvement had nothing to do with
getting hurt or not getting hurt. He had no need to commit, so he didn't. There was no Mrs Right for him because
that was a complication he didn't need. He was perfectly
fine as he was, unlike Pamela Morgan, who wanted more.
Unlike her daughter, who probably wanted more as well.

'And you think that's what I'm doing?' Alice bristled
but there was a charge in the atmosphere that was thrilling. And she couldn't peel her eyes away from his lean,
dark face.

'You want more of *me*...' He sat back and allowed his
eyes to roam over her; lazy, indolent, darkly sexy eyes that
made her body burn. 'Why don't you stop running scared,'
he murmured, 'and just take what you want? Take what
you can't tear your eyes away from.'

'You are the most conceited person I have ever met in
my entire life!' She was breathing fast and, God, he *knew*
exactly how she was reacting to him. Knew it and liked it.

'You want to touch...I can feel it. Do you know why?
Because it's the same for me. I want to touch you too. Why
do you think I spent hours driving down here on the spur
of the moment?'

But you will never get hurt, Alice thought. *You can
touch and then walk away unscathed...*

But was that enough of an excuse to run scared? If her
mother could get involved with someone, as Gabriel had
told her, then why couldn't she? How many times would

she spend her life running scared when faced with the possibility of getting hurt?

And yet the thought of any other man having the same impact on her as Gabriel was far-fetched, almost beyond belief. He wasn't the gentle kind of guy who would gradually entice her back into the world of trust and love, the kind of guy she had vaguely pinned her hopes on finding at some point in her life. He was the dynamic, darker-than-sin, more-dangerous-than-the-devil kind of guy who would take her places she had never been and leave her broken-hearted when he walked away.

'Shall we go?' he asked huskily and Alice nodded mutely.

'This was never the plan,' she said shakily, once the bill had been paid and they were standing outside the restaurant.

'What was never the plan?'

'This. Me. You… It's not a good idea.'

'Life is about taking risks or else what's the point? I've spent my life taking risks. I wouldn't be here today if I hadn't taken risks.'

'What do you mean?'

Gabriel laughed but his dark eyes never left her face. 'Maybe one day I'll explain.' He threaded his fingers through her hair and tugged her towards him. 'Do you want me to kiss you? Because if you don't then this is your opportunity to say no and to walk away, and we can go back to playing our game of "it never happened".'

'Kiss me…'

Alice lost herself in that kiss. It was a crazy place to be doing this because she might get spotted. It was a small village and the fact that her mother had spent much of her time there confined to her house didn't mean that there weren't many locals who didn't pop in for chats, to see how she was doing, to have tea or the occasional supper. Any one of those locals would have hot-footed it right back to Pamela Morgan with tales of her daughter being seen outside that new Italian restaurant kissing a man.

But she couldn't resist. She breathed in his woody, clean aftershave, felt his firm, cool lips plundering her mouth and her body curved into his. She looped her arms around his neck and tiptoed to meet his searching mouth.

'I'm only thinking...' he broke apart to say in an unsteady voice that didn't sound at all like his '...about your reputation when I say that we need to take this somewhere else.'

'I don't want you to stop.'

'And I don't want to...' With his arm slung heavily over her shoulder, they half-ran to his car and picked up where they had left off the second the car door was slammed shut.

It was teenage, 'back row of the movies' stuff. That was what it felt like to Gabriel and he loved every second of it. He had never done that back-row kissing business; he was making up for lost time. If her teenage years had been spent caretaking her mother and being strong on her behalf, his had been spent digging himself out of the hole into which he had been born, forging a life for himself that would be strong enough to ensure that he would never have to look back or go near that hole again.

The fact that they had so much in common was a fleeting thought that was almost immediately buried under the urgency of his response.

He felt under the red jumper and found the obstruction of her bra, but made short work of that by plunging his hand under it, pulling free one breast that popped out, nipple already standing to attention, tightening to a rigid peak as he teased and pinched it into arousal.

The car was parked at a distance from the other random cars and the tinted windows meant that they were cocooned, protected from any curious eyes, not that there seemed to be many people around. Protected enough for him to feel comfortable raising her jumper so that he could cover that pulsing nipple with his mouth and suckle on it until she was whimpering and panting, spreading her legs in delicious invitation.

They were never going to make love in his car, he thought, wondering if his body would be able to tolerate the short drive back to her house without relief. But he could enjoy her for a bit longer, suck for a little longer on that circular disc.

With a groan of frustration at not being able to go the whole way, he flung himself back against the seat and groaned.

'I need a bigger car!'

Alice could still feel the warmth of his mouth on her breast. She pulled down the jumper, as regretful as he was and as desperate to get back to the house so that they could finish what they had started.

Making love with her mother a couple of doors down? True, her mother slept like a log, often with the aid of a sleeping tablet, but still... Never in a million years would Alice have seen herself as the kind of girl who would be driven to have sex with a guy in her bedroom because she just couldn't hold off. Since when had she ever been the kind of girl who lost complete control? *Since she had gone to Paris*, was the answer that came immediately to her. Since she had made love to him. Since she had discovered a carnal side to her that was insatiable...

Before he could fire up the engine, she reached across and fumbled with his zip.

More teenage stuff! Gabriel didn't bother to try to resist. He'd lost the ability to play it cool. Right now, what he needed more than anything else was release.

He unzipped the trousers and manoeuvred himself so that he could pull them down, along with his boxers. The cool night air was soothing, but not nearly as soothing as her mouth…

CHAPTER NINE

THE HOUSE WAS in darkness by the time they arrived back. Pamela Morgan was already in bed. It was nearly eleven and she was accustomed to retiring early.

Gabriel had no idea how he had managed to get back without going into one of the hedgerows by the side of the road. He couldn't concentrate. The woman next to him had taken his self-control and shredded it into a million pieces.

Yes, she had relieved some of that ache…

He caught his breath sharply, remembering the glorious feel of her mouth on him as she drove him to his climax. The release had been…indescribable.

Now he wanted more, much more.

He would have brought her to her own orgasm, would have put his hand and his fingers where his mouth would not have been able to go because of the confines of being in a car, but she had stopped him, breathlessly telling him that she wanted him in her bed.

Now, as she unlocked the front door with shaky fingers, he placed his hand over hers.

'We could wait,' he said gruffly. 'I don't want to. Hell, I would take you by the side of the house if you let me… But I don't want this to be seen as an abuse of your mother's hospitality.'

'I'm beginning to think that I haven't given Mum enough

credit for being a grown-up,' Alice said ruefully. 'She's probably been waiting for me to bring a guy home but not confident enough to come right out and say anything.' She pushed open the door and held her finger to her lips in a signal to keep quiet, then giggled softly, because she felt light-headed, young and very happy.

And he hadn't been able to get her out of his head! She gave herself full permission really to drown in that admission, really to luxuriate in it.

Paris had been an adventure but she had managed to convince herself that it had somehow been acceptable because she had been abroad...just a passing fever. But this was *really* an adventure because she was here, in her stamping ground, making a conscious decision to do something because it felt inevitable and somehow *right,* even if it was wrong.

She couldn't explain it, even to herself. She just knew that she had to sleep with him, had to follow this through to the bitter end, however and whenever that might arise, even if it meant saying goodbye to her job in the process.

They went up the stairs silently. Sure enough, when Alice looked to her right there was no light on in her mother's room. She turned left, thankful that her bedroom was at the end of the narrow corridor, and she pushed open the door, heart beating so fast she had to make herself take deep breaths just to steady her spiralling excitement.

She could still taste him in her mouth...it was a turn-on.

'Your bedroom?' Gabriel asked, looking around him. Moonlight streamed through the window, picking up bits and pieces of her belongings: a rocking chair in the corner, on which sat an oversized, battle-weary stuffed teddy bear; furniture that looked as though it had never been made to last; a dressing table with some framed pictures on it.

'Don't talk.' She pressed her body against his and her eyelids fluttered closed as he slipped his hands under her jumper. This time he undid the bra and she released him for a few seconds so that she could pull the bra and jumper over her head so that she was standing in front of him, half-naked.

'You're so damned beautiful...' Gabriel cupped her breasts with his hands and massaged them, rubbing the pad of his thumbs over her nipples as he did, and felt the breath catch in her throat. He leaned down and kissed her neck, then licked it, then nibbled his way up to her mouth so that she could lose herself again in another of those devastating kisses.

Alice pushed her hands under his jumper, seeking the warmth of his flesh. He had small, flat brown nipples and she teased them just as he was teasing hers and felt him respond.

Slowly they made their way to her bed, unable to break apart from one another, kissing and holding each other and stumbling a little in the dark until her knees made contact with the side of the bed and she fell, taking him with her and stifling another giggle.

This was nothing like the luxurious bedroom they had shared in Paris, with its fabulous, ridiculously lavish *en suite* bathroom. This was basic, but in fairness at no point had she detected anything condescending in his reaction to her mother's house.

He pushed himself up and removed his shirt and jumper, tossing them carelessly to the ground, then he stood so that he could rid himself of the rest of his clothing—trousers, boxers, socks. His shoes, he had already kicked off.

Then he was back on the bed and very, very slowly he unzipped and pulled down the black trousers, taking her lacy briefs with them at the same time.

He tossed them aside with one hand while using the other hand to part her legs.

Not that there was any need for him to do that. Her body knew just what to do when it came to making love with him. She settled back with her arm resting lightly over her eyes, her limbs wonderfully loose.

She knew what he would do. He knew how much she loved it, loved having him down there between her legs. And still, the moment his tongue flicked against her, she couldn't prevent the soft moan that escaped her lips.

She arched up, pressing herself against his questing mouth and exploding inside as he licked and teased the throbbing bud. She was so wet for him, so turned on, so ready to have him thrusting inside her—but he continued to torment her by remaining where he was, lavishing all his attention on her aching core and the soft, tender skin of her inner thighs.

Then he moved up to her breasts, leaving her on the very brink of coming. He drew one nipple into his mouth and played with the other, smiling against her body as he felt her desperate efforts to make as little noise as possible.

'Wrap your legs around me,' he commanded.

But first he had to get hold of protection, which was damned difficult, because it involved finding his wallet and then going through it in the darkness, while they both craved release.

He never took chances. Ever. It was one of the most significant things that indicated just how he felt about any woman being able to tie him down. Even at the very height of passion, he would rather walk away from making love than take a chance on an unwanted pregnancy.

Why was that? Didn't everyone, to a greater or lesser extent, have within them the urge to procreate, to see their bloodline continue? She had never asked him, had known that that was a boundary line she would cross only at her own peril.

Yet he knew everything there was to know about her now. He knew about her miserable childhood, the effect it had had on her, on her mother... He knew about the circumstances that had driven her mother to take refuge within the safety of her house, trapped by her own fears. He could make sense of her and the way she was from the background she had had.

But it was a one-way street because there were still so many questions that remained unanswered about *him*.

Alice knew that this was just one of the many reasons why it was so dangerous to get back into bed with him. She knew that somewhere in the very core of her, but she couldn't help herself, because fighting against that knowledge was the realisation that she would rather end up hurt than end up regretful for not having taken the chance.

With Gabriel, the probability of pain was always right there, huddled close to the promise of pleasure.

All her thoughts led somewhere, but she couldn't follow them, because the way he was touching and caressing her made her mind shut down.

She did as she had been told and wrapped her legs around him and felt him push inside her, big and hard.

Then he built up a rhythm and she stifled her moans against his neck. She was so highly charged that it took considerable effort to try and hold off so that they could dovetail their orgasms, but she did it, and they came together.

He reared up, stiffened, the muscles in his shoulders bunched as he gave himself over to wave after wave of pleasure, the same pleasure that was taking her into another dimension. But the questions that had been nibbling away slid out of the shadows and began nibbling again.

Was this all he was capable of—sex? Did he really have no interest in ever having a family, something and someone more permanent in his life? And, if sex was all he wanted, then why was that? She had seen so many facets of him and yet the way he was pieced together still eluded her and she would dearly love to find out more.

The pitfalls of being in love: it made you want to know everything about the person you loved. In Gabriel's case, that would be a suicide mission. That was something she felt in her bones, with gut instinct.

'That was…amazing,' he murmured, sliding off her, but immediately lying on his side and turning her to face him.

Alice murmured agreement. Making love had been a conscious decision on her part, but she could still feel tension seeping in, tension at knowing that, whilst she was fully committed to their relationship, he wasn't.

It was amazing for him because he had got what he wanted. What he felt was the satisfaction of the victor and it was a satisfaction that was not going to last for ever.

But she wanted for ever.

Her own innate honesty compelled her to recognise that she would take what she could for as long as it was on offer because any bit of him was better than nothing. Yet the prospect of the end would hang over her like the hangman's noose so that every time they made love, every time she laughed with him, felt his arms around her, it would be tarnished with a sense of sadness. She could feel the weight of the end on her shoulders even before what they had actually ended.

She wondered what difference it would make if she only knew what made him tick. Or at least *some* of what made him tick.

'Tomorrow's Sunday,' she said, languid and content after their love-making. 'What will you do? Head back up

to London? My offer still stands to pop in to Harrisons in
Exeter before I come back to work on Tuesday.'

So cool, Gabriel thought, so composed. No hint of any
nagging or trying to wheedle him into staying on...

The perfect woman—but he couldn't help feeling a little
piqued at her offhand attitude. A tiny amount of posses-
siveness might have been nice, he found himself thinking.
After all, hadn't he made this trip down here just to see
her? That in itself had been a break in tradition.

'What are *your* plans?' He turned the question back
at her and Alice rolled onto her back and stared up at the
ceiling.

Her plans were what they always were—except tomorrow, she conceded, would include an informative chat
about the new man in her mother's life. Aside from that,
as long a walk as Pamela Morgan could handle, maybe
even making it into the village for tea, some light television and then she would make something for their supper.

What she would have really liked was to have Gabriel
all to herself, but that was an admission she would never
make...

'I shall relax.'

'In that case, I might relax here with you,' Gabriel
drawled, propping himself up on one elbow and tracing
the outline of her rosy pink nipple with his finger until the
prominent bud stiffened in automatic response.

However cool she might be, her body was as hot as his.

'Really?' Alice injected a note of surprise into her voice.
'Surely you must have plans for the rest of the weekend?'

'As of this moment I consider them cancelled.'

'Because you'd rather spend time down here?'

'It's a beautiful part of the world.'

'Yes. Yes, it is.' She noticed that he couldn't actually
admit to wanting to put whatever previous plans he had

made for his weekend on hold because he preferred to spend the time *with her*. 'Although you might find it a bit boring,' she said truthfully. 'I don't suppose you have much experience of living out in the countryside...'

'I prefer the push and shove of the city. Suits my personality.'

'Aggressive?'

'You said it.' He idly inclined his head to suck her pouting nipple before settling back into his former position, looking at her, his face only inches away from hers. She had the clearest brown eyes fringed by sooty, thick, dark eyelashes; eyes that were open and wary at the same time. 'So, sell me this part of the world,' he invited lazily. 'Do your best pitch. Wax lyrical about walks in the open fields, tea and scones at somebody's little shop—maybe a barn dance later at the village hall.'

'Would you be interested in doing any of those things?'

'I think we can eliminate the barn dance.'

'Now, that just makes me wonder if there's one on at the village hall,' Alice teased. 'I can't see you enjoying walking in the open fields or having scones at the local tea shop, either,' she mused. 'Are you one of those city people through and through? Born and raised, would never leave it for longer than five minutes?'

'Not exactly.' He stiffened fractionally. This was where the caring, sharing had to stop.

'In the country, then? Don't tell me your parents used to drag you out for Sunday walks? My mum always made sure we went out on a Sunday afternoon for a really long walk, whatever the weather. She liked being out of the house, away from Dad. Although she always had to make sure to get back in time to prepare his tea if he happened to be at home. The closer we got back home, the more anxious and nervous she would become. Course, those walks stopped when I turned eleven, when I preferred to hide out in my bedroom studying or reading.'

'I didn't have country walks—or any walks, for that matter,' Gabriel heard himself say roughly. Restlessness surged through him, making him feel uncomfortable in his own skin, and he sat up and swung his legs over the side of the bed. Then he strolled towards the window, across which the curtains hadn't been drawn.

Stark naked, with his back to her, he gazed broodingly out to the dark shapes of fields, hedges, a copse of trees to the right in the distance.

That, Alice thought, was the sound of a door being firmly shut in her face. She sat up and pulled the duvet up to her chin.

Eventually he turned round but he didn't walk back to the bed.

'So…' A slashing smile lightened the passing shadow that had crossed his face. 'What exciting things shall we do tomorrow?'

'Aside from the barn dance? We can have a walk, perhaps with Mum, and then look around the village—go to that little shop for tea and scones…' *Enjoy pretending that this is a normal relationship…*

'But first thing in the morning,' she told him firmly, 'I will have a chat with Mum.'

Pamela Morgan was up bright and early the following morning but the coffee was still hot, ready to be drunk, when Alice made her way down.

Her thoughts were still all over the place. She had slept with him; she had lost the fight to put her feelings behind her and allow the common sense that had always ruled her life to take over, as she had told it to. As she had *needed* it to.

He didn't know the depth of her feelings—which was something, she supposed—but he knew how much she wanted him and, now, her life had been laid bare for his perusal. Not content with keeping what they had to London, he had invaded her life here in Devon…

And revealed things she herself hadn't even known about. Which showed just how much he had managed to ingratiate himself with her mother.

But then, he was the man who didn't have to try; the man who could move mountains with a smile, with a lazy turn of his head, with just a look…

'Alice, dear…! How was the meal last night?' Pamela Morgan was beaming. 'You never told me what a lovely man your boss was! Such a looker…'

'We need to talk, Mum.'

'Do we, dear?' But there was a tell-tale flush in her cheeks as she sat down opposite her daughter and fiddled guiltily with her coffee cup.

'A man…? A suitor…? You never said…' Alice had been hurt when Gabriel inadvertently had told her about a man in her mother's life but that hurt hadn't lasted. How could it, when her mother's eyes were glowing as she chatted happily and with relief about Robin, her friend's cousin who had moved to the village to start up his own small landscaping business. He was wonderful…they had so much in common. They had only seen each other a handful of times but thanks to him she had managed to venture more and more into the village; he had even taken her to see his company, which was still in the process of being set up.

Alice was dazed.

'But why didn't you say anything to me all this time?' she finally asked, but she knew why.

'Just a few weeks,' Pamela said uncomfortably. 'And

I knew you'd try to warn me off him, my darling, and I would quite, quite have understood, but...'

But she, Alice, her loving daughter, would have disapproved, would have issued stern warnings, would have dished out helpful advice by the bucket load, and in the end would have stifled anything that had a chance of surviving. Her mother had wanted to take a chance and she would have been afraid that her daughter would have killed that chance dead.

Alice wasn't hurt, she was mortified. Years of helping to prop her mother up had turned her into a hard-edged young woman who had allowed her own disillusionment to colour her behaviour.

Gabriel's entrance half an hour later helped to lighten the glum introspection into which she had been plunged and, with an unerring ability to cut to the chase, the first thing he said to her as they were walking out of the house was, 'You're upset. You spoke to you mother...and...?'

It was not yet nine-thirty but already the sun was warm and the open fields were bathed in the clear, unencumbered light so typical of the countryside where buildings and pollution didn't cloud the view and sully the air. He realised he didn't mind it. He quite liked it, as a matter of fact. A change from urban life.

'Do you really care?' Alice turned to him. The breeze ruffled her hair, blowing it across her face. She was slender and coltish in a pair of faded jeans, an old baggy jumper and a pair of walking boots.

'I'm interested; of course I am.' Gabriel refused to give in to qualifying what he felt. Naturally he cared if she was upset. He wasn't a monster. And, yet, when was the last time he'd actually *cared* whether some woman was upset or not? Had he been that bothered when Georgia had flounced into his office and thrown a hissy fit because she couldn't take no for an answer?

He had been irritated but he certainly hadn't been upset. Nor had he ever been curious about what happened or didn't happen in a woman's life. As long as they gave him what he wanted, he was absolutely fine and he always, but always, made sure that his conscience was clear by being upfront with them. Life was so much simpler when you made sure you didn't get wrapped up in complicated emotional situations that would always end up leading to dead ends anyway.

He had nothing to give and wasn't interested in trying to break that mould.

But he sensed that she had asked a leading question and he knew that he should repeat his honest, upfront, 'don't look to me for anything but sex and a good time' talk—just in case she had forgotten. And he *would*...but later...

He was *interested*. He didn't *care* but he was interested. Two completely different things, as far as Alice was concerned.

'And she's got a boyfriend.'

'Good for her.' Gabriel slung his arm over her shoulder and breathed in the fragrant, floral scent of her hair. God, what was it about this woman that drove him nuts? 'I want you so much right now that it hurts.'

Alice pulled apart and stared at him then she rolled her eyes and laughed. 'Is sex *all* you think about, Gabriel?'

'It's pretty deserted out here...'

'I was talking about my mother!'

'And I'm listening. I just want to touch you a little while you talk...' He slipped his hand under her jumper and circled her narrow waist. 'Tell me you don't like that.' Up ahead, the fields were broken with clumps of trees. It was an idyllic, picture-postcard scene. 'You're not wearing a bra. I like that...'

'I usually go bra-less when I'm down here. I don't have enough to warrant wearing one twenty-four-seven...'

'You have just the right amount.' He pushed up the jumper, ignored her half-hearted attempts to swat him away and gazed down at her small, pert breasts tipped with their rosy pink nipples.

Her breathing quickened as he rubbed the sensitive tips with his thumbs until they were stiff and aroused.

This was her wild adventure. She had fallen in love with the wrong man and had thrown caution to the winds because her heart was ruling her head. She *knew* that he was only in it for the sex, for the good time, but it was so hard to bury the part of her that wanted to find out where they were going, whether there was the slightest chance that he might want more than just sex.

He gently pulled down her jumper; his hand went to the button of her jeans, then the zip, and she gave a little shocked yelp as he began tugging down her trousers.

'We can't.'

'Why not? All right; we can find somewhere a little more private under the trees, although there's no one around. Is it always this deserted?'

'You need to get out of London a little more.' She was damp and hot as they walked hand in hand towards the nearest bank of trees. 'There're lots of places like this out here. It's quiet, peaceful. That's why Mum decided that she wanted to move here. It was restful after living in Birmingham. I also think she wanted to be as far as she could from any ugly reminders of her marriage.' She pulled him towards her and stretched up to kiss him, fingers clasped behind his neck, their bodies pressed so tightly together that she could feel the hardness of his urgent, demanding arousal.

'Lying down might be a little uncomfortable,' Gabriel said, but he had to have her. Nor did he want the substitute of her hand or her mouth. He wanted to be inside her, *needed* to be inside her.

'Then let's forget about it and stroll back down to the village,' Alice teased as she stroked his cheek and watched the fire blaze in his dark eyes. 'We could have that scone and that cup of tea. Tea can be very refreshing…might cool us down…'

'You're a witch,' Gabriel said in an unsteady voice he barely recognised. He tugged down the jeans, told her to step out of them.

She kept the jumper on. Being half-naked like this, with her bottom half-exposed, felt decadent.

'Now, legs apart,' he commanded.

Having him down there, standing perfectly still when she wanted to collapse because her legs felt as wobbly as jelly, was exquisite agony.

He explored her, taking his time. It surprised him that he'd never made love outdoors and he thought that next time he would make sure they brought a rug with them.

Next time? Yes, there would be a next time, because he couldn't get enough of her…

Their love-making was basic, wild and hard. He hoisted her up so that her legs were wrapped around him. She could have been as light as a feather.

The sensation was intense. Her buttocks clenched as he drove her down on him and she came over and over, splintering into a thousand glorious pieces.

Afterwards, the walk into the village was languorous. Sated, Alice had never felt happier. It was almost as though they were a normal couple—ducking into shops, laughing at some of the souvenirs on sale, stopping to buy ice-creams. Mr and Mrs Average on a day out.

What a joke! She reminded herself that they certainly were not Mr and Mrs Average, or Mr and Mrs *Anything*.

He certainly wasn't average! In fact, he cut an impressive and madly exotic figure next to his paler counterparts as they dipped in and out of the shops. People stared. He didn't seem to notice, but *she* did. Women of all ages stole glances; wondered; maybe thought that he might be someone famous.

For the first time in her life, Alice felt as though she had stepped out of the shadows and become a person in her own right, someone who wasn't so surrounded by barriers, that she could be free to just...*be*.

They had a very long lunch in one of the three pubs in the village and it was only when they were emerging that she bumped into one of the ladies whom she knew visited her mother on a regular basis.

Alice had never socialised with Maggie Fray, but they had met on a couple of occasions, and now the older woman stopped and looked at Gabriel with twinkling, knowing eyes.

'So this is the young man your mother says you talk so much about.' She held out her hand with a smile while, mortified, Alice tried to shrink away from the grey, inquisitive eyes.

'My boss...' Alice said in a thin, high voice, but minutes before they had been holding hands and that begged the question of what exactly the relationship between boss and secretary was.

The older woman's smiling eyes seemed to be making all the right assumptions.

'Well,' she said comfortably, 'you two seem to make a very good match. And I know your mother would love to hear the sound of wedding bells in the not too distant future!'

On a scale of one to ten of hideous conversations, Alice rated this one at somewhere around twelve. She barely heard the rest of whatever Maggie was chattering about.

How much had she told her mother over the many weeks that she had been working for Gabriel?

A lot. They were accustomed to sharing. Even if she had made a big effort to play down the way she felt about Gabriel, she unknowingly would have given the game away because her mother could read her the way no one else could. Her mother would have been able to interpret her hitched silences, the expression on her face whenever she mentioned his name, the number of times she talked about him and the number of times she didn't…

Her arrogant, self-centred, infuriating, egotistic boss who was also brilliant, inspiring, unbelievably smart, charismatic and funny. And the fact that Gabriel had shown up at the house, uninvited, unannounced and apparently with no other purpose but to see her, would have given credence to whatever fairy stories her mother had been concocting in her head.

'People in a small village are inclined to gossip,' Alice said weakly as Maggie disappeared towards one of the shops, having given them a cheery wave goodbye. 'It's very annoying. Because…er…most of the time, what they say has no basis in truth *whatsoever*…' Alice couldn't bring herself actually to say out loud what the older woman had said. To mention that word 'wedding' would open a can of worms and she didn't know how she would be able to stuff them back in.

Gabriel was ominously silent.

He should have seen this coming. He had warned her

off but he should have clocked that there was something intensely vulnerable about her.

'Vulnerable' should have hit his radar and generated the automatic 'no trespassing' response, but somehow his guard had been down. It was what novelty and lust did when they came together—a lethal combination.

'What the hell was the woman talking about?' He beeped open the car and climbed into the driver's seat, but he didn't start the engine. Instead, he waited for her to follow suit, and then he turned to her with a cool, unreadable expression.

'I told you...' A hint of defiance had crept into her voice. 'In a village there's always gossip. Maggie is one of my mother's friends and somehow she's managed to get hold of the wrong end of the stick.'

'Because *out of nowhere* your mother somehow gleaned, erroneously, that we're...*what* Alice? About to tie the knot? Walk up the aisle? Start believing in fairy stories and building castles in the sky?'

'You're so bloody *cynical*!' she exploded. 'And *no*. I haven't been telling my mother *anything*. I'm not so stupid that I'd fall into the trap of thinking that you're there for anything but the short term, Gabriel!'

'I'm not going to get into a pointless argument with you over this.' He started the engine and began driving slowly away from the village.

Alice couldn't credit that they had been making love not so long ago. She couldn't believe that she had been so stupid to think that, if she blanked out the fact that she was hopelessly in love with him, everything could tick along nicely until such time as...what, exactly? He got bored? Became indifferent?

Was she so desperate that she would abandon all her principles just to steal a bit more time with him?

Was it any wonder that he had become so lazy over the years when women like *her* allowed him to get away with doing exactly as he wanted?

She had fallen under his spell and been mesmerised. She had slept with him in Paris; had kidded herself that she could walk away and carry on working for him without any repercussions. But there *had* been repercussions. She had been so aware of him, so acutely *sensitive* to his presence, that she had scarcely been able to function.

He had found his way to the very essence of her and he had taken up residence there.

She had never been an addict of anything in her life, but she had become addicted to him. Was that why she had fallen right back into bed with him— because he had happened to show up at her house and had told her, in that dark, dangerous, sexy voice of his, that *he hadn't been able to get her out of his head?*

Or maybe she had been injected with some sort of crazy, dare-devil urge because her mother—her always hesitant, always careful mother; her mother to whom she had preached the good sense of *not getting involved with a man* because *just look at what she had ended up marrying*—had had the courage to embark on a relationship?

Or was it just a combination of things that had galvanised her into the worst choice she had ever made in her entire life?

She could find a million reasons to justify why she had done what she had done, but in the end what it amounted to was that she had climbed onto a roller-coaster ride and now it was time to climb off.

Gabriel Cabrera was the equivalent of an extreme sport and she just didn't have the constitution for it.

She blanked her mind to the thought of the endless days and nights ahead of her which would not contain *him* in them. She would have to hand in her notice, find work somewhere else.

'It would only be a *pointless* argument,' Alice half-shouted, 'because you don't want to have it! And, just so you know, I'll be handing in my notice first thing on Tuesday morning.'

'You're being ridiculous!'

'And that being the case,' she continued as her anger, mostly with herself, spilled over, 'I might as well tell you that you may think you're being fair by warning women off you, just in case they get it into their silly little heads that you might actually have *a heart* buried there somewhere, but you're not. You're just taking care of your conscience. You don't want to have to try at anything that isn't work. You'll end up a lonely, sad man with stacks and stacks of money but no one to share it with!' She was staring at his profile which could have been hewn from rock.

There was no getting through to him. Why hadn't she been strong enough to wise up to that before? Dig deep below the charm, the looks, the charisma and the formidable intelligence and there was…*nothing*.

Those glimpses of gentleness, tenderness, vulnerability had all been an illusion. She shut the door on any other interpretation. She was shaking like a leaf and kept herself as rigid as a plank of wood to control emotions that threatened to burst their fragile containment.

'And on that note,' Gabriel drawled, 'I'll drop you back to your house. There will be no need for you to return to work. You can consider that little speech of yours a suitable letter of resignation.'

They were at the house. She hadn't even been aware that he was driving.

He reached across to click open her door and she drew

back, horrified at how her body reacted even now, when everything was falling apart.

'If there's anything personal that you need to take from your office,' he said coolly, 'then you can get in touch with Personnel. They can forward it to you.' Their eyes tangled and Alice was the first to look away.

She couldn't find room in her head to accommodate everything she was feeling: the horror of the end; an overwhelming sadness; self-recrimination.

'There's nothing I want to take with me.' Her voice betrayed nothing of what she was feeling. She stepped out of the car, walked towards the house and she didn't look back.

CHAPTER TEN

FROM WORKING IN one of London's landmark buildings, Alice's life returned to normality with a deafening thud.

One month after she had walked away from Gabriel, she was now back in employment, working as a legal secretary in a small solicitor's firm in the outskirts of London. She had gone from towering views of the city to the nondescript view of the back of a local supermarket car park. She had moved from the most exciting man on the planet to a middle-aged chap who handled small cases and apparently took himself off to play golf twice a week.

The highlights had grown out of her hair and Paris and everything else seemed like a dream.

She had not heard a word from Gabriel and, much as she had not expected to, the hope with which she awoke each morning turned into the sour disappointment that went to sleep with her each night.

Walking back to her house, her mobile phone rang and, when she picked up the call, it was from her mother.

Pamela Morgan's recovery was coming along in leaps and bounds. In fact, treatment with the therapist had been reduced to once a month. Now that her love affair was out in the open, it seemed to be all she could talk about, and Alice, having met the man in question, had to concede that her mother was in safe hands.

Time had moved on, her mother had told her; she was in a different place from the one she had been in when she had married.

The implication was that Alice should have reached a similar conclusion—that time had moved on and she was no longer the girl growing up in a scary, dysfunctional family or the girl who had had a brief fling with someone who'd turned out not to be Mr Right.

The implication was that there was a time and a place to be careful and Alice was young enough to take life by the scruff of the neck and take chances...

Alice had not become bogged down in discussing her situation. She could have told her mother that she had taken enough chances with Gabriel to last a lifetime, but she kept quiet.

Now, her mother was talking to her about a holiday she planned to go on and marvelling that her life had been turned around so dramatically.

Alice listened, contributing here and there as she stepped off the bus and headed back to the house.

It was an overcast, muggy day and although it wasn't dark, far from it, she was still surprised that the lights in the house were all off because she knew that Lucy would be in, getting herself ready for a hot weekend in Venice with the guy she had been seeing for the past few months.

It was a little after eight. Overtime was not expected but she had stayed on until just after six and had then gone out for a quick drink with two of the other girls from the office, who had a Friday-night routine in which she had been immediately included.

She was exhausted.

She let herself into the house, dropping her bag by the door, and heading for the kitchen whilst removing her lightweight summer jacket at the same time.

With the lights all switched off, the downstairs of the house was bathed in a grey twilight that Alice found rather soothing, so she didn't bother turning on any lights, instead carolling up the stairs to let her house mate know that she was home.

The last time she had arrived home unexpectedly without loudly announcing her arrival, she had discovered Lucy and her loved-up guy in the sitting room about to embark on a compromising position, and Alice had been horribly embarrassed. Since then, entries were always as noisy as possible.

The last person in the world she'd expected to see was in the kitchen chair and he'd been there for the past hour.

Gabriel had been driven to seek her out. The past month had been hellish, his worst possible nightmare. He had been unfocused, unable to concentrate and in a permanently foul mood. People had scuttled in the opposite direction the second they had heard him striding through the office, on the hunt for someone on whom he could vent.

He had even broken his own personal record by dating six women, none of whom had progressed beyond polite conversation over dinner. In their company, he had spent an inordinate amount of time checking his watch.

He had refused to give in.

Hell, the woman had burned him off not once, but *twice*!

It hadn't helped that he had not managed to find a suitable replacement for her. He was on secretary number three and the omens were not good.

He had cursed himself on more than one occasion that he had been lenient enough to let her leave without duly working out her notice. On reflection, he should have made her do the two weeks required.

His nights had been no better than his days. Work had

failed to do what it should have done, distracted him from thoughts he neither liked nor invited.

He missed her.

He missed everything about her. He missed the way she spoke her mind; the way she laughed; the way she looked at him. He even missed the way she smelled. And all that was why he was now where he was—sitting in her kitchen, having despatched her friend, who had allowed him entry only after a questioning the likes of which hadn't been seen since The Spanish Inquisition.

'I thought you'd never get back. Where the hell have you been anyway?' Casual voice to mask his far from casual emotions. Controlled but barely breathing.

About to reach for a bottle of water from the fridge, something to quench her thirst after three glasses of wine, Alice nearly fainted in shock at the sound of that voice which had haunted her for the past month.

She spun round and stared at the figure in the chair, speechless.

Her legs turned to jelly; she collapsed into one of the kitchen chairs facing him and just *stared,* unable to believe the evidence of her eyes.

'I've been waiting for over an hour.' Had she been out with a guy? No. If she had, she surely wouldn't have returned home so early. Maybe she'd been on a date which had been a disaster. He enjoyed the thought of that. He had been on enough disaster dates himself.

'Gabriel…' It was the only thing she could find to say. Her mouth was dry and her heart was pumping so hard that it felt as though it would burst.

'Your house mate let me in.'

'Lucy.' This was a surreal conversation. She couldn't peel her eyes away from him. He looked…haggard. He was still in his suit but he had disposed of his tie and the top two buttons of his white shirt were undone. For a man who always managed to look carelessly elegant, he was dishevelled.

'Right.'

'Why are you here?' Alice knew that she should sound firmer, angrier, more resolute. Her voice was thin and reedy and she cleared her throat and continued to look at him in the half-light: beautiful. Even drawn as he was, he was still the beautiful guy who had lodged like a burr under her skin and refused to budge.

And suddenly the anger that should have been there rose to the surface—because, she thought, she must not forget that this was the same emotionally lazy man who had walked away from her without a backward glance because he had got it into his head that she might, just might, be interested in more than just a romp in the sack!

This was the same guy who *had nothing to give.*

'No,' she said coldly. 'Let me guess why you're here. You can't get to grips with any of the secretaries you've had to replace me. Well, if you think that I'm going to come along and do a good deed by handing over, then you're wrong. I'm not going to be doing that. You've wasted your time, so you can leave. You know where the front door is.' She was trembling and she wrapped her arms around her to steady her nerves.

Gabriel had never lacked self-confidence. It was what had propelled him upwards, had given him the drive to leave his past behind and the confidence of knowing that he could do it. Right now his confidence had gone on holiday. He was shaken by the sensation of someone standing on the brink of a precipice with one foot hanging over the side and no safety net to catch him if he fell.

'I didn't come to try and get you to come back to work,' he said hoarsely. 'Although your replacements haven't been any good, as it happens.' That last offering failed to generate even a hint of a smile.

And why would she smile? She had given and he had taken and, in return, had stayed true to his lifelong motto of giving nothing back.

He had been a prize idiot.

'In that case, why are you here, Gabriel?'

'I'm here…because…because…'

He was stammering. Since when did the invincible Gabriel Cabrera *stammer*? But she wasn't going to let any sprigs of hope infiltrate the barriers she had been trying so hard to rebuild around herself.

'Forget it.' She clenched her jaw and forced herself to look at him, to meet his black stare without flinching. 'I'm not about to climb back into a relationship with you.' She laughed shortly at how lacking in veracity that was, because it had hardly been a 'relationship' by anybody's standards! '*Relationship.*' She spoke aloud, her voice thick with self-mockery. 'What a joke. As you've proudly told me, you don't *do relationships,* do you, Gabriel?'

'I said that. How was I to know that fate can sometimes have a nasty habit of laughing at all your good intentions?'

'Forget it, Gabriel. Forget all the fancy words.' Restlessness invaded her body like a sudden burning itch that needed to be scratched. 'Have you run through a few of your pocket-sized dates and decided that you weren't quite through with me just yet?'

'I've missed you. Have you missed me? Tell me that you haven't and I'll walk out of this house and you will never see me again.'

As ultimatums went, that one went beyond the barrier. She didn't *want* him here, did she, invading her life all over again? Smooth talking his way back into sex because of *unfinished business*…did she? But she hesitated because the finality of what he was offering terrified her. She might not really have expected to see him ever again, but now she could see that she had stupidly *hoped,* because her love was so strong that it seemed incredible that she could be left with nothing overnight.

Now she knew that if she turned away this time she really would never see him again. Fragile hope would be killed dead.

'Well?' Gabriel prompted shakily.

'So I missed you! Big deal. Does that change anything?'

'You're the first woman I've ever missed.'

'Am I supposed to be flattered by that?' But she was. And she didn't want to be any more than she wanted to feel the racing of her heart; any more than she wanted to be moved—stupidly, idiotically *moved*— by the way he was looking at her with eyes that were somehow naked.

She didn't want any of that because none of that changed the man that he was, a man who was incapable of giving.

'You can't give anything, Gabriel,' she said, reconfirming that simple fact to herself just by voicing it out loud; reminding herself that she had been sucked in not once but twice and that she was not going to be sucked in again. 'And you have *no right* to barge into my house, to sweet-talk my friend into letting you in so that you can sit there and start spinning stupid stories just because I didn't give you what you wanted!'

'I'm not here to spin stupid stories.'

But Alice was in full flow. Memories rained down on her, memories of how much she had given and how little had been returned. 'You're empty inside, Gabriel! One stupid three-second conversation with someone you met in the village and you took off in a hurry. The merest shadow of a hint that you might have been expected to provide more than just inventive sex and you couldn't escape fast enough! And now you have the nerve to come here and talk about *missing me...*'

'I get it, Alice. I should have got it sooner, but I get it now.'

'Don't you *dare* try and make nice with me for your own benefit!' *And stop looking at me like that...* 'Repeat: you can't commit! You can't even plan a month ahead with any woman because you might need to run away long before then! You don't just want to make sure that you don't put down roots, you want to make sure that you don't even leave *footprints!*' She was shaking like a leaf, all the hurt and anger bubbling up inside her.

'Oh God, Alice. Do you think that I don't know that every single word you're saying is true?' He sat forward, angling the chair so that he could lean his forearms on his thighs. Still hunched, he raised his eyes to look at her. 'You were right when you once accused me of being emotionally lazy. I am. Was. Always have been.'

Was...? Hope flared, as persistent as a weed and as tenacious as ivy. Drained by her outburst and by the desperate range of emotion surging wildly through her, she remained silent, her breathing heavy and laboured, as though she had run a marathon. She wanted to drag her eyes away from him but found that she couldn't, any more than she could stop her heart from opening up like a wound that had only been scabbed over, bleeding all over again. 'I want you to leave,' she whispered. 'You need to leave.'

'Please. Let me just... It's hard for me; just hear me out. There's something you probably don't know about me.... No, there's something you *definitely* don't know about me...' That standing-on-the-edge-of-a-precipice feeling was back, but he didn't care whether he fell or not, or whether there would be a safety net to catch him or not.

Nothing could have been worse than the past few weeks without her.

'I was dragged up in foster homes. You told me your story, and maybe I should have repaid the confidence, but confiding is something I've never done. I've never known how. It's something that's sucked out of you when you're a kid in care. You learn to get tough fast. So, I've never told anyone my story.' He smiled crookedly at her. 'Until now.'

'Foster homes?' She shook her head slowly.

'Correct. No privileged upbringing. No upbringing to speak of, in actual fact. Just driving ambition and, thankfully, sufficient brainpower to turn that driving ambition into career success. But someone consumed with driving ambition, someone who had to fight to clamber out of a crappy background. What can I say? There was no space left inside me for sharing—I wanted money and everything that comes with it because it made me invincible. And for a long time that was exactly what I was: invincible.' He looked at her, reading her thoughts, stalling them at the pass. 'No fancy words, Alice. Just me. Being open.'

'And then what happened? You were invincible...' She tried to imagine a youthful, defiant, angry Gabriel and her heart constricted. He had erected the same defences as she had, but his had been made of steel and he had never let them down, and she could understand why. 'You're not going to get me back into a non-relationship with you with a sob story,' she said half-heartedly because she knew that she should still be protecting herself.

'I don't want to get you back into a non-relationship.'

'Oh.' Disappointment seared through her like a blazing inferno. So he had come to explain himself. That was something—that he had thought enough of her to tell her about his past—but she wanted so much more...

'I need you to see that for me giving in a relationship

had always been a non-starter. I was dependent only on myself, the way I always had been for my entire life, and I had no intention of allowing anyone in to share that space. But you came along, Alice, and bit by bit you chipped away…'

'You never hinted that you wanted anything more from me than a sexual relationship.'

'I refused to believe that I did. I've been a fool, Alice.' He dared to reach out and was shaken with relief when she allowed him to twine his fingers through hers. 'I should have known that you were different, and not just because you were taller than the women I usually dated. Hell, I was *that* thick.' Another of those crooked smiles made her toes curl and did all those things to her body that she had become accustomed to whenever she was around him.

'I went from looking at you, to wondering, to fancying and then to wanting you more than I'd ever wanted any woman in my life before. And somehow, in the mix, came all that other stuff…'

'What other stuff?'

'The wanting…the craving…the needing and the loving…'

'You *love* me?'

'And I never even recognised it for what it was.' His voice was strangely shaky when he next spoke. 'So I haven't come here to restart a non-relationship, as you called it. I've come here to ask you to marry me so that we can start just the sort of committed, fairy-story, walk-up-the-aisle relationship I never thought I'd have. Because, Alice Morgan, I find that I can't live without you. And if you can't give me your answer now—and I'd understand, because I've been a hellishly poor excuse of a lover—then you can think about it.'

He stood up and he was already at the kitchen door

when her legs did what they had been programmed to do and sprinted after him.

'Don't you *dare* go anywhere,' she said breathlessly, her eyes shining. She flung her arms around him and held tight. 'Because I love you, Gabriel Cabrera. So, yes, yes and yes! I want to marry you. I want to be with you for the rest of my life.' She looked up and her eyes were glistening with unshed tears.

'No fancy words?'

She laughed and sniffed and laughed again. 'I had my own barriers,' she confessed, dragging him back to the kitchen table, but this time when he sat down, she sat on his lap because she just needed his arms around her. 'You know all about my dad, and I guess I always thought that it was safer never to let go, never to put myself in a position where I could be hurt. I was so determined that you wouldn't get under my skin. I'd categorised you in my head within days of working for you, and somehow I thought that made me *safe*.' She stroked his hair, kissed his dear face and submitted when he kissed her back, tenderly, lingeringly.

'You mean if I was a bastard then you could never fall for me...'

'But, bit by bit, that image started to melt and fall apart. And then there was Paris...'

'And then there was Paris...'

'I just...got lost in you, Gabriel. It was like you got hold of my heart, and I was terrified, because you'd laid down all those ground rules of yours; because I knew your views on commitment... I decided that the only way to deal with it was to back right off. I thought that, if I backed right off, there just wouldn't be the glue to keep you attached but it was too late.'

'Hell, Alice, it was too late for me as well. You were in

my head all the time and, idiot that I was, I never stopped to ask myself why I love you, Miss Morgan—and I can't wait for you to become Mrs Cabrera.'

'I can't wait either.' Her world had opened up the day he had entered it and she felt like she was soaring high when she thought about the whole bright future taking shape in front of her. 'I want you to hold me and never let me go, because I'll never let *you* go.'

* * * * *

MILLS & BOON®

Want to get more from Mills & Boon?

Here's what's available to you if you join the exclusive **Mills & Boon eBook Club** today:

✦ *Convenience – choose your books each month*
✦ *Exclusive – receive your books a month before anywhere else*
✦ *Flexibility – change your subscription at any time*
✦ *Variety – gain access to eBook-only series*
✦ *Value – subscriptions from just £1.99 a month*

So visit **www.millsandboon.co.uk/esubs** today to be a part of this exclusive eBook Club!

MILLS & BOON®

Need more New Year reading?

We've got just the thing for you!
We're giving you 10% off your next eBook or
paperback book purchase on the Mills & Boon
website. So hurry, visit the website today and type
SAVE10 in at the checkout for your exclusive

10% DISCOUNT

www.millsandboon.co.uk/save10

MILLS & BOON®
MODERN™

POWER, PASSION AND IRRESISTIBLE TEMPTATION

A sneak peek at next month's titles...

In stores from 16th January 2015:

- **The Redemption of Darius Sterne** – Carole Mortimer
- **Playing by the Greek's Rules** – Sarah Morgan
- **To Wear His Ring Again** – Chantelle Shaw
- **Claimed by the Sheikh** – Rachael Thomas

In stores from 6th February 2015:

- **The Sultan's Harem Bride** – Annie West
- **Innocent in His Diamonds** – Maya Blake
- **The Man to Be Reckoned With** – Tara Pammi
- **The Millionaire's Proposition** – Avril Tremayne

Available at WHSmith, Tesco, Asda, Eason, Amazon and Apple

Just can't wait?
Buy our books online a month before they hit the shops!
visit www.millsandboon.co.uk

These books are also available in eBook format!